From the Eye
of
Kate Henry

From the Eye
of
Kate Henry

MEMOIRS OF A NEGRO SLAVE WOMAN

John Y. McClure

author·HOUSE®

AuthorHouse™
1663 Liberty Drive
Bloomington, IN 47403
www.authorhouse.com
Phone: 1-800-839-8640

Director of Photography
MICKY PICKENS, JOAT-LLC

Published by AuthorHouse   03/15/2012

ISBN: 978-1-4685-4315-5 (sc)
ISBN: 978-1-4685-4314-8 (hc)
ISBN: 978-1-4685-4313-1 (e)

Library of Congress Control Number: 2012900716

This book is printed on acid-free paper.

Contents

Foreward

The Memoirs of a Negro Slave Woman Named
'Kate Henry'

This story began with a knock on the front door and four strange looking people standing there. One was a lady and three were men.

"*Hello there Miss, are you Mrs. Amanda Henry?*"

"*I sure am and let me guess, you're the folks that wrote me a spell back about the history of my plantation, aren't you?*"

"*Yes Ma'am the strangers responded.*"

"*Well won't you fine folks come in and rest for a spell as I get ready to talk to you.*"

They all went inside and sat in the parlor.

"*Well now let me first introduce myself and all of you fine folks can properly introduce yourselves to me.*"

"*My name is Amanda Henry and I'm sorry to say that my husband, Mr. Rob Henry passed away more than eight years ago. Now what's your name Miss?*"

"*My name's Sandra and these young men with me are my three sons. This one on my left is my oldest and his name is Jessie; the tallest*" in the bunch, and my second oldest is named Daniel; the splitting image of his father, and this one in the front of me is my youngest, my precious little baby boy and his name is Herbert. I guess he's no baby, he's twelve years old.

"All of you speak and say something nice to this fine lady here."

The young men all properly greeted Ms. Amanda.

"Well now Miss what you say your name was again?"

"My name's Sandra, Sandra Dean Bell."

"Ms. Bell I must say you got three fine, charming and handsome looking sons."

"Thank you so terribly much Mrs. Henry; that was just so kind of you to say."

"Oh, now you ain't got to call me no Mrs. cause I ain't married no more. I'm a widow woman since my husband."

"Oh! Ms. Henry dear I'm so sorry to hear tell!"

"Oh it's alright and Sandra you and your husband still together?"

"No we ain't Ms. Amanda, he's gone on to glory just like yours and that's one of the reasons why I'm out here now trying to do writings about historical plantations. I'm doing all I can to try to feed my three sons and I'm barely making a living out here."

"You poor thing, believe me I sure do know that it's hard making a living without your man. Would any of you like some coffee or tea?"

"Thank you Ms. Amanda. That would be just downright neighborly of you."

They all sat down and began to talk.

"Ms. Amanda we heard that your plantation once was the biggest plantation in this entire county and your plantation was the first plantation that ever had a trained slave negro doctor." Is all that stuff true?"

"It's all true."

"Ms. Amanda, if what you're saying is really true, would you explain to us the story of how in the world such a thing as this ever happened?"

"It sure is true but to be honest with you Ms. Sandra, my memories and recollections have gone and gotten bad considering my age. I would have a hard time recollecting all of the good gossip and side tickling stuff you want to hear about."

"Ms. Amanda you mean to tell us that we came way out here and we ain't even going to get a story? Ms. Amanda, what are we going to do?" "When we wrote you, you wrote us back and told us faithfully you would help us get our story!"

"Now, now Ms. Bell even though I done got feeble and can't hardly, see, hear or recollect anymore, I still do try to always keep my word. A body's word is a body's bond you know."

She looked all of them in the eye and said, "I know I told you all in my letter that I would help you and I will do everything just like I promised. Before my husband passed away there was a slave woman that we owned and cared for. This slave woman can tell you anything you want to know. She has a memory as good as Mr. Henry when he was alive." "Ms. Bell do you think your father or your husband's father *could have done something that could have made God mad?"*

"I wonder if God hears slave's prayers or not, and if they got souls like white folks."

"Ms. Bell that sounds so silly of you to even say such as that."

One of Sandra's boys asked Amanda why she said such a thing like that bout his ma. He went on to say to Ms. Amanda that she couldn't say nothin to make him believe God hears no slaves prayer.

"Herbert, boy ain't you being a bit disrespectful to Ms. Amanda?" *"Son, you better go and apologize before I go and whip you up and good like."*

"Oh, it's okay Ms. Bell I understand." *"Come here son let me hug you."*

She hugged him and he began to laugh and told her he was terribly sorry for what he said.

"I know son, believe me child I know. Let me tell you a little story about a slave that once followed a preacher around on his crusades. This preacher couldn't preach worth a dime but he had a slave that he took around with him and when the slave would lay his hands on sick folks they would instantly get well."

"What you mean by instantly?"

"I mean the moment he would touch them, the same moment, they would get well."

"Ms. Amanda how sick would the folks be?"

"Well Daniel, some of the folks would be crippled, crazy, blind and their sight would come back and everything."

"What about crazy, demon folks and stuff?"

"*Jessie God can do anything!*" *My husband, the late Rob Henry had a limp in one of his legs for years from rodeo riding and the slave touched him and his leg got straight and he never did limp anymore.*"

"*Ms. Amanda, how did we ever get on all of this nonsense?*" "*What did you tell us was this slave woman's name?*"

"*I told you before her name is Kate.*"

"*Ms. Henry just what is this slave woman supposed to be telling us anyhow?*"

"*She's going to tell you some stories about this plantation's past.*"

"*Such as what, Ms. Amanda?*"

"*Kate can remember and tell you everything beginning from when she first came here, met her husband, had a son and named him Joeson. How her son helped and cured thousands of white folks and slaves.*" "*Tell you how he and our own white town doctor, Doc Waters, became friends.*" "*She'll have you laughing about the town's madam, Ms. Hawkins.*"

"*She can tell you how they made liquor and medicine at the same time.*" "*Kate used to make me laugh and cry all at once when she told me how she reunited with her lost sister and brother.*"

"*Kate Henry remembers the tallest tales ever told about a terrible Tornado and my husband's pa's beginning and his death. "Don't forget to get her to tell you how me and Rob first got hitched and how my husband once shot a man in his rear end about her son.*"

"*But before you start talking with her let me warn you she's quite a feisty thing and don't you try to play her for no fool cause she does know and believe in God."*

"Ms. Amanda, where can we find this Kate lady?" "Just go out of my front door and go into any of my fields and ask any of the folks you see and they'll tell you."

The writing group was told where to find this slave lady on the rundown Henry plantation. They all headed to the back of the main house. There was a path that ran about half a mile into the woods.

Finally they saw the little shack of a house. In one of the front sides was a mid-sized garden that looked as if it had been tended constantly. It had several rows of corn with runner beans climbing the stalks and crowder peas between the rows.

There were tomatoes with fishing cane sticks propping them up and several rows of cabbage, watermelons, cucumbers, onions, sweet potatoes and more and even a few grape vines growing in several of the rows all alone. On the left of the shack was a rock cemented well with a grass rope and wooden bucket. Her house was sort of fancy looking for slab planks. It was held up on slab rocks on all four corners.

You could look completely underneath this house and see chickens scratching under it. In her front, back and side yards were several cats with their kittens walking in and out of her front door at will.

Two old rough looking hounds were tied to a nearby tree. Before the group stepped up to the door, they had mocking grins on their faces because of the outward appearance of the house but when they knocked on her door and stepped inside, their jaws dropped at the site of the gorgeous home.

Kate was a very frail old looking woman but she had a very sweet and kind sounding voice. She allowed the group to enter her house and rest themselves with as much as she had. Kate was interviewed by the group and asked would she tell them the story of the plantation as best as she could remember. Kate, now a very old and feeble woman, agreed to tell all she could remember.

The group first wanted to hear how her son had become a doctor. Kate was a bit skeptical about telling her tale to the perfect strangers. She asked them would they please give her a copy of the reading after they were finished writing it.

The group insisted no slave knew how to read and what would she do with it seeing it would have no pictures. Kate angrily refused to help them and she politely asked them to leave her house. After leaving Kate only chuckled and said to herself, *"White folks think they know everything about us black folks don't they. Now where did I put my book and where is that page I left reading from."*

The group asked Amanda if she would please persuade Kate to tell them the story. Amanda told them if they wanted a story from Kate Henry they all need to take themselves and apologize and reconsider whether or not to give her what she wanted. They considered Amanda's advice and followed through with promising her a copy of the writing.

The group attentively listened as the old lady spoke. She began telling her tale by telling them about how her son, a slave, had become a plantation doctor. Daily the group would be at Kate's shack from sun up until sun down until her tales had all been told.One of the young men questioned Kate one afternoon before they left for the day about whether she believed in God. *"Yes sir I sure do,"* she *replied.*

"Do you believe in Jesus?"

"Sure I do sir," she said.

"Well then can you tell us what color you think Jesus is?" *"Is he white like us or is he black like you?"*

Kate looked blank at the question at first but suddenly she spoke up and said, *"Sir when a body gets out of bed in the morning and drinks them some milk and they get them a biscuit and some butter to swipe on the biscuit and they eat and get full, sir they don't rightly give a mind if the milk and butter came from a white, black, brown or spackled cow."*

The next day she was asked the same question but this time she gave another answer. "Sir if a body is thirsty and ask someone for a cold drink of water and they give it to them, they ought not to give a mind whether the water came from a well or a river."

May the good Lord bless you all.

1

The Henry Plantation

Somewhere down south in the early 17th century the sun beats down upon row after row of tall corn, boll weevils feasting on morsels of cotton and Master Henry's plantation.

This plantation was the biggest and the oldest in the county. Master Henry raised cotton and more cotton, corn and more cotton, summer and winter wheat and more cotton, peanuts and more cotton, cows and more cotton, hogs and more cotton, and loads of horses and more cotton. He owned over two hundred field slaves. His eight white row masters and two foremen helped him run the plantation and such.

Master Henry was a tall white man standing about three hands higher than a horse's bridle with raggedy crow black hair and dark gray horse eyes. He had very bad sun beaten skin with several marks and scars. A noticeable scar was under his left cheekbone where he had been beaten by a married man. His stomach had been stabbed twice because of bar room fights.

His smile was pleasant despite the numerous fights; he still had all of his teeth. He had a slight limp when he walked from being thrown and kicked by different horses and bulls numerous times. Despite all of the stomps, kicks, and bruises he still loved the critters.

Master's wife was a fancy looking gal, but that was all she was; just fancy looking. She didn't know anything much about high society life. She was always gone from home pretending that she was all knowing about how to be and act like a big society lady.

This is also the home of a beautiful Ethiopian or perhaps she was an African housemaid. She was about mid high with big shinny hazel brown eyes. Kate Henry, that's me, was the young maid's name. She had been bought by Mr. Henry and was a favorite house gal. My job was to cook clean and take care of the Master's house.

Another slave arrived at the plantation, Old Joe was his name. Joe was the name his Ma and Pa's Master who let the midwives give him a name about six months after his birth and Henry was his Master's surname. All slaves were allowed to keep their birth names but they later took their Master's last names.

When Joe had first came into the new plantation he was shown all of the new surroundings and he met the other slave folk. He was given a place to sleep and three changes of clothes and an old pair of boots that he was tickled to death about, even though they were about two or three sizes too big. Old Joe only wore shoes after a hard frost or snow fall, when spring and crop time came the shoes had to go.

Master put Old Joe out in the fields working the rows. He was no good at working the rows because he was not your typical slave; he had special furniture making skills. His craft was second to none. He was always fighting and causing trouble with the other slaves.

Master Henry got sick and tired of taking Old Joe out to the woodshed and introducing him again and again to the black snake whip. All he would do was scream, yell and cry only to return back out yonder in the fields and fight again. So Master finally gave up and sent him up to the big house. When Old Joe arrived at the big house and laid eyes on me he began to smile.

2
Just Listen To Um

The group was treated to some of the best acting they had seen in those parts as Kate retold the events prior to Master Henry's death.

Master Henry laid near death and was attempting to prepare his son to take over the plantation.

[Master Henry]   *"Da plantation is doing just fine now, son all yous got ta do tis jus keep things gowing. rite."*

[Mister Rob]   *"But pa ya knows I don't no's nothin bout running no dat blamed plantation; all I's no's ta do tis how ta ride and break horses."*

[Master Henry]   *"Yeah son I knows but son your pa is a-dying."*

[Mister Rob]   *"Oh pa now please don't go an says that cause yous' no's I care fo ya, and loves ya."*

[Master Henry]   *"I no's son, but somebody got ta carry on here boy when ya pas gone boy."*

[Mister Rob]   *"Pa why don't ya get one of ya other two dat blamed sons?"*

[Master Henry]   *"Son ya knows good and well fo ya dat blamed self that both of dem rascals ain't nothin but drunks and needier one of got sense enough ta do nothin but drink, fight, gamble and chase old nasty whores. Anyhow both of-um all ways spiting in da wind."*

[Mister Rob]   *"Yeah pa and I knows who dem dun gone and got it from to!"*

[Master Henry]   *"Look a here boy don't ya be gone and a sassing me now boy."*

[Mister Rob]   *"Ok pa I's sorry . . . but . . . Pa whys didn't ya calls and send fur me and have me fetched sooner so I's could be teached and properly learned this here job."*

[Master Henry]   *"Cause . . . boy . . . yous twas all da dat blame times gone out yonder somewheres trying ta be a dat blamed old Rodeo cow poke or something stupid, of all things . . . and me and none of ya folks ever knew where ya twas 'Sambo' and ya never showed no never mind ta let ya folks know where in tar nations ya twas and*

that's why boy or I meant ta say
'Sambo'."

[Mister Rob] "Now pa my name ain't no 'Sambo'
and ya no's I hate ta be called
that name."

[Master Henry] "Well ya act like a 'Sambo'
ta me 'Sambo' . . . boy what else
ya gonna ask ya pa?"

[Mister Rob] "Why not my sister?"

[Master Henry] "Why not your sister boy
ya must be crazy ain't ya, that
there gal ain't got sense enough
ta even get out of da rain, little
lone how ta runs a fine plantation
like this here and any who I's dun
gone and told ya befo that ya my
one and only whole white son!"

[Mister Rob] "I's no pa, ya dun gone and
secretly told me befo dat all ya
other younguns twere half and half
but me."

[Master Henry] "Oh gone say it 'Sambo'!"

[Mister Rob] "Say what pa?"

[Master Henry] "Ya know what boy."

[Mister Rob] "Ya mean that ya younguns were
part white and part colored."

[Master Henry] "Don't call my chillen
colored boy, cause dem tis . . .
black."

[Mister Rob] "That ain't nothin pa cause
most of da other slave masters
here and bouts got mixed up chillen
too . . . but pa!"

[Master Henry] "But . . . nothin . . .
boy when I's dun gone and put my
head back in da dust ya better take

over this here plantation . . . or
else."

[Mister Rob]   *"Or else what pa?"*

[Master Henry]   *"Or else I's gonna come
out of my grave and hunt ya day
and night . . . ya hear me boy?"*

[Mister Rob]   *"Yeah pa I's here. Ya know pa
at least ya don't call ya other
chillens what ya used ta call your
other slaves!"*

[Master Henry]   *"Well son befo I had one
of dem kind of little old black
chillen on my own, I did call dem
some pretty bad names ya know, but
now I get a big lump in my neck and
a tight knot in my gut when I say
that word."*

[Mister Rob]   *"What word is that pa?"*

[Master Henry]   *"Oh ya know son da word
ni . . . ni . . . Oh I just can't
say it bout my own."*

[Mister Rob]   *"Pa I bet ya didn't get no
lump in your neck and a knot in
ya gut, when ya twas getting dems
mas . . ."*

[Master Henry]   *"What boy . . . I dun told
ya "Sambo" ya better stop sassing
ya pa boy."*

[Mister Rob]   *"Pa if-ans I's gotta take over
this here plantation when in tar
nations do I start?"*

[Master Henry]   *"Yous really needs ta
starts rite now boy."*

[Mister Rob]   *"Pa I would rather ya had
called me 'Sambo' or that N-word
that gives ya that lump and knot,*

than ya had said that. But why now pa?"

[Master Henry] *"Don't ya but pa me boy look-key here son,"* (cough, cough, cough, hack, hack, hack, cough).

[Mister Rob] *"Lay easy now pa . . . lay easy pa . . . don't get so upset now! Here take some of ya medicine."*

[Master Henry] *"Huh I don't want none of that dat blamed old nasty, tasting medicine."*

[Mister Rob] *"Why not pa its good fur ya."*

[Master Henry] *"Shot boy cause I want me a drink from that there little old brown jug I's got under this here bed."*

[Mister Rob] *"Now pa ya knows for sure that ya needs ta leave that their stuff alone."*

[Master Henry] *"Oh shet up boy and mind your poor old sick and dying pa and hand me that their jug under this here bed of mine."*

[Mister Rob] *"Now pa ya know if Kate your house gal comes inside of here's and sees ya guzzling down that junk her gonna be real mad at you-ons . . ."*

[Master Henry] *"Hand me that jug "Sambo" befo I get out of this here bed and beats yous with a knotted plow line . . ."* (cough . . . cough . . . hack . . . hack . . . cough . . .)

[Mister Rob] *"Now . . . now pa if ya quiet down some and ifs ya promise not* ta talk so loud maybe I'll give ya a little drink if ya just pipe down a little bit, just pipe down some pa . . . my goodness."

[Master Henry] "Ok! Boy hurry up befo Kate comes in ta check me."

[Mister Rob] "Where's ya glass at pa so I can pour ya a drink?"

[Master Henry] "Boy ya sho ya my son, cause Son ya sho don't know nothin bout drinking whiskey do ya knuckle head . . . ya don't waste clean glasses fo drinking good corn liquor, ya just turn da jug up and drink straight from that their little old jug . . . And hurry up boy I can hear Kate coming."

[Mister Rob] "Where's da jug at pa?"

[Master Henry] "Under da top of da bed stupid!" (He looks on top of da bed). "Not on top of da bed stupid . . . under da bed, under da bed . . . ain't no ways ya my son."

[Mister Rob] "Oh! I's sees it pa and I's got it pa . . . a he . . . he."

[Master Henry] "Hurry up boy and pull da cork I can hear Kate coming closer, she's coming threw da kitchen and she'll be here in a few . . . What in tar nations ya doing 'Sambo' I thought I dun gone and told ya ta give me a drink and here ya is drinking befo me . . . put that jug down boy and . . ."

[Mister Rob]   *"Oh hush pa here takes ya a swig."*

[Master Henry]   *"Hurry up Rob give me da jug . . . she's almost at da doe . . . AAAA Man, Lawd that twas good . . . (hack, hack, hack, cough, cough, hack . . . .) Hurry up Tom hide da jug boy, hide da jug."*

The door flies open and Kate stands in the entrance.

[Kate]   *"Master Tom I's dun heard ya!"*

[Mister Rob]   *"Heard what?"*

[Kate]   *"I's dun heard."*

[Mister Rob]   *"Let me guess Kate, yous dun gone and heard Master coughing?"*

[Kate]   *"No sir, I's dun heard . . ."*

[Kate]   *"Little Rob!"*

[Mister Rob]   *"Ok, I give up. I know ya heard me giving pa a drink."*

[Kate]   *"No, I was just tryin ta tell ya pa that I's heard that da doctor was coming ta sees hem and by da smell of this here room, da doctor must'uv beat me here and changed Master's medicine cause da other medicine on hems breath didn't smell that ways befo. I's don't knows what kinds of medicine that there doctor dun gone and gives ta Master but it sho do stink and smells just like old liquor ta me. I don't see what in da world anybody in their rite mind wants ta drink that stinkin stuff fo."*

[Mister Rob]   *"Now Kate a little corn liquor ain't gonna hurt nobody, right pa!"*

[Master Henry]   *"Yeah son, sho ya rite and even da doctors says tits some good medicine at times fo different ailments."*

[Kate]   *"Now Master, ya knows good and well liquor ain't no kind of medicine."*

[Master Henry]   *"Why not Kate?"*

[Kate]   *"Cause Master medicine tis suppose ta makes ya well and not sick; I's member how yous be heaving at one end and running at da other and holding ya old head and guts after guzzling that junk; rats want drink that old puke and if an outhouse fly lights in it dem somehow starts ta fly backwards."*

[Master Henry]   *"Now Kate I think ya just needs ta hush up cause ya being just down rite disrespectful ta ya Master . . . rite Rob?"*

[Mister Rob]   *"That's rite pa!"*

[Kate]   *"Yeah sir Master, Im's sorry. Cause I's don't knows if-ans Master knows it but that when I's twas cleaning up da other day their twas a little brown jug with a white fishing cork in it and tit somehow had walked and hid itself under hems bed. I opened da jug and took a smell and almost passed out from da stink; I's dun hurried up child and put da fishing cork* *back cause of da offal smell . . . I's twas gonna toss it out, but I's knows ta fust ask and tells Master. This here room smells just like that jug dun gone and turned over. I's don't knows what in da world causing that here smell in this here room . . . so I's gonna open that there window so some fresh air can comes in chere befo Master gets stiffened and starts coughing again. Now what was you's saying Mister Rob?"*

[Mister Rob] (Smiling) *"Well Kate I was saying Oh, Oh yeah, ya da doctor did beat ya here and changed pas medicine."*

[Kate] *"Oh yeah."*

[Mister Rob] *"Kate look under pas bed and see if ya can see that there jug ya twas talking bout."*

[Kate] *"Yes sir Master!"* (Kate takes a good look but says) *"No sir Master I's don't sees it."*

[Mister Rob] Mister Rob was setting on Kate's blind side, in a chair next ta his pas bed) *"Look again gal ya must'uv over looked it . . ."* (as he was talking he was taking his foot and sliding it under his pas bed.)

[Kate] (She looked again). *"Oh there it tis, I wonder how in da world I didn't sees it at fust."*

[Master Henry] *"I guess ya just twas half looking that's all gal."* (winking his eye at his son).

[Kate]   *"I's guess so."*

[Kate]   (She held da jug up in her hands and lightly shakes it). *"Nothins left."*

[Mister Rob]   *"Is anything left in da jug?"*

[Kate]   *"No sir it ain't, even da corks missing and it twas spilled over just now when I's dun picked it up so's I's guess it must have spilt and dun dried up, but I's swear it twas full yes-ditty when I's twas cleaning under Masters bed . . . I's wonder just what dun gone an happened; I's no Master can't climb under hems bed, can ya Master?"*

[Master Henry]   *"No I's sho cant Kate and if-ans I's could I's wouldn't causing I's knows you-ons don't wants me ta do nothin like that."*

[Mister Rob]   *"Well Kate what dose ya thanks dun gone and dun happened to's that thur medicine stuff that twas under yonder in that jug?"*

[Kate]   *"Well Mister Rob I's just don't knows what in tar-nations dun gone and went with it. What in creations do yous dun thinks dun happened ta tit?"*

[Master Henry]   *"I thanks its dem old ghost yawl slaves be telling bout."*

[Kate]   *"What ghost Master?"*

[Master Henry]   *"I's guess dem ghost and haunts that eat and still my food and stuff . . . now I guess dem dun* *gone and starting drinking liquor ta hum!"*

[Kate]   *"Who and what tis ya yacking bout Master?"*

[Master Henry]   *"Oh ya know says Master, dem ghost yowl told me bout that stole my darn chickens . . . that totally vanished and somehow disappeared . . . and my biggest smoke hams and beef side meat from my locked smoke houses? Oh a he-he, says Kate, maybe it twas dem dun old ghost after all, that dun gone and dranked up that thur medicine stuff in this here jug."*

A knock came on Master Rob's bed room door.

[Kate] *"Who tis it?"*

A known voice is heard on da other side of da door and it says

[Doc Jones]   *"It's me Doc Jones and I dun come by ta sees how Old man Henry's getting along and I dun gone and over heard yawl outside da doe."*

[Kate]   *"Come right on in Doc Jones sir how's ya been getting along ya self. Well Doc Jones sir, I's can imagine yous dun cames way-ouch-chr ta only zamin "Master" but now I's thinks ya needs ta checks out hems son to; but ya just wasting ya time and effort!"*

[Doc Jones]   *"Why in tar nations would ya go and say such a thing as that there gal?"*

[Kate]   *"Cause Doc Jones sir I's can already tells ya befo ya check dem . . . dat dem both filling and dosing just find!"*

[Doc Jones]   (Doc Jones questions and asks Kate). *"How in God's creation ya know that . . . gal ya ain't no doctor tis ya?"*

[Kate]   *"Well sir, I's ain't gotta be no doctor or medicine man ta knows cause buy da smell of dems breath and if-an dems thinks I's believe in ghost dem both gotta be drunk. And po Master hem dun always said, after us dun told hems bout dem dun ghost eating hems meat and drinking hems apple cider hems always says well let da darn ghost have it cause hems don't wants ta ever drink or eat behind no ghost I's gonna toss this here empty jug out and break it . . . Ok . . . Master Rob?"*

[Mister Rob]   (Master Rob answers Kate and says) *"Ok Kate dos whatever ya thinks right and da good Lawd wants ya ta do."*

[Kate]   (Kate headed fo da door chuckled and smiled). *"Oh look . . . . it did have a glass or so left! . . . sees ya Doc"*

[Doc Jones]   *"Ok Kate."* (Doc laughed)

15

3

Master Tom Henry's Death

Although the sun was out there was a dark cloud over the plantation. All the slaves were not working in the fields today because they were attending a religious service at the plantation on sacred grounds.

"Rocks of Ages, cleft for me, let me hide myself in Thee. Let the water and the blood from thy wounded side did flow. Be of sin the double cure," was the melody that echoed and whispered in the air that afternoon while the lovely yellow haired young lady was singing. Some of the older slaves were asked to come up and sing one of their field songs.

"Swing Low Sweet Chariot A Band Of Angels Coming After Me: Coming Fourth To Carry Me Home. I Looked Over Jordan And What Did I See A Band Of Angels Coming After Me. Swing Low Sweet Chariot Coming Fourth To Carry Me Home."

The young and old slave ladies cried as the sweet melodies were laid on mournful ears. Deacon Day was asked for remarks and he prayed "The Lord's Prayer", as it had never been prayed before. All the slaves were allowed to come around and pay their last respects to the remains.

The plow boys passed by with hung down heads and hats in their po hands . . . . some with silent words, . . . others whispered, "rest in peace Master." The house maids and field women were cryin and wringing their hands saying . . . "bye Master," "bye Master" . . . "we's sho gonna miss ya" . . . "we's sho gona miss yous."

One little girl that Master would let ride his horse filled her apron with tears as she raised it to her face. She sobbed, "Lawd takes good care of Master and I'm gonna see him again someday." After the funeral she didn't talk for three days.

The preacher came around and read from the good book, the 23rd Psalms. Six men came forth three on each side of the wooden box and lifted up its weight to the back of the wagon. The wagon was driven by a man in a black suit with a large brim black hat. The wagon stopped with about two or three little maids carrying flowers. Where the wagon finally stopped there were about five men just finishing up digging a hole in the ground as tall as a man's eyes and half as wide as a man is tall about six feet deep and four feet wide.

The six men that loaded the box on to the wagon came walking up and took the box off of the wagon. They took ropes and let the box down into the hole. Three other slaves listened as the parson said his ashes to ashes and dust to dust and they began to throw dust and a hand full of flowers in the hole on top of the box.

A few folks and friends from town cried. All Mister Rob could do was just stand and hang down his head and say, "Pa's gone, Pa's gone . . ." Mr. Little Tom fainted. Somebody had to hold Missie Mae Tae up and their other brother was already dead from yellow fever. Master Tom Henry had gone to join his son. Master Tom Henry is now dead. The men that dug the hole began to put shovels of dirt back into the hole.

All the town folks and friends drove their wagons and rode their horses back home and the slaves were off in the fields for seven days.

The very next day, Mister Rob Henry took over the plantation and became the new master. He had been living with his pa for about two and a half years before his pa died. His pa had asked him to start taking charge before he died. While old man Tom was alive most of the slaves didn't care that much for him, but death brings out the best in most of us.

Before he died he called all of his slaves to his bedside and talked to them and told them that he knew that he was dying and would they please forgive him of any wrong he had done to any of them. They all said they forgave. He made his peace with man and his God before he died.

4

Peek-A-Boo

Kate's eyes lit up and a great big Kool Aid smile dawned her face as she remembered the day they brought Old Joe home to the Henry Plantation. Old Joe had three different Masters. He once was called Joe-Farmer, Joe-Smith, and now he'd be called Old Joe Henry.

Kate shared how the new plantation had Rob's hands full all of the time. His crops were always plentiful however he still held to his love for horses and he bought and raised a few dozen for riding and some for breeding and selling. He also needed more help with the large amount of work; therefore he made plans to buy some new slaves.

The new slaves would be purchased from another slave owner named Jamison Smith. Mr. Jamison was a big store owner and he sold all types of fancy clothes for men and women and he traded all sorts of glass and fine dishware. His store was renowned for some of the finest pots and pans money could buy. He also was a dealer and maker of all sorts of fine furniture.

Young brides to be couldn't resist the temptation to buy all types of wooden tables, chairs, beds, and such. Jamison had dozens of slave men and women folk working for him, and he had trained them how to stitch and sew fine and fancy dresses and tailor made suits for men. Slaves knew how to heat iron core, beat and pour out the fanciest pots and pans you ever did see. Joe was one of his many slaves that knew how to take wood and whittle it into fine masterpieces.

Jamison had too many slaves and not enough buyers of his fine products. Master Henry had gone to Smith's fine store alone and saw all of the fine work that had been done and he simply fell in love with a couple of the fine hand carved and painted rocking chairs. The chairs were hand rubbed with rope cord weaved seats and backs.

The store owner had carvings of little pretty painted wooden things to put on the mantle, such as horses, dogs, cats, chickens, birds and critters. Rob had purchased a few of these things to surprise his wife Amanda.

During the transaction Master Rob made a deal on the spot to purchase several of the slaves that Jamison was going to auction off. One of them was Old Joe. They all were bought one year to the day after the death of Old man Henry, Rob's pa.

None of the new slaves were purchased for making things. They were all bought for the sole purpose of working the rows and caring for the fields. As Joe began his new job he was a hard worker and certainly earned his keep. He was no good at working the rows cause he was always fightin' and causin' trouble with the other slaves.

Master Henry got sick and tired of taking Old Joe out to the wood shed and introducing him again and again to the black snake whip. All he would do was scream, yell, and then promise to be good and cry only to return back out yonder in the fields and fight again. One day he was sent to the big house to repair a broken chair arm.

After he knocked on the door it was opened by a lovely black faced, hazel eyed lady with well-groomed braids on her head. She cleaned his new Master's house and cooked in the kitchen. When they first saw each other it was infatuation from the first moment. This beautiful creature asked if she could help. He told her he was sent up to see bout fixing Master's chair. She showed him the chair that had the broken right arm handle. He took it and introduced himself and asked her named.

She responded that her name was Kate and she was pleased to meet him. They engaged in conversation and Kate didn't hesitate to ask him if he had a wife and kids. Boy was she glad when he said he wasn't hitched now although he had been hitched before. Then it was Joe's turn to get the goods on Kate. He was glad also to learn that she wasn't hitched.

Joe asked Kate if she had any whittling knives and saws that he could use. Kate asked him to follow her to the barn out yonder where all the saws and stuff like that were kept. On the way out to the shed she fetched a small whittling knife from the kitchen.

After they walked past several animal stalls, they came to a little ladder leading up to the hay on the second floor of the barn where the hay loft was. Kate first began to climb the rails and Joe puts both hands around her waist in an attempt to help her up the steep steps.

When she reached the top she called down to Joe to come up and help her open the top of a big box. After opening the box, Joe saw that it was full of all sorts of working tools, hammers, saws, chisels, and wedges and such. Kate told him look and take whatever he needed. Joe reached in and picked out several tools he might need to repair the chair.

All of the slave workers lived together. There would be four or five living together in their cabins but married folks lived alone. The field and house folks just didn't get along. The field hands felt like they were the Master's real slaves and they called the house slaves Master's 'boys or girls' whichever. Because of the dislike for the house slaves, they were kept in different cabins in order to prevent the field slaves from jealously beating and killing them.

Kate lived in a cabin by herself but Old Joe had to sleep with three other boys. Two of the boys he slept with were house boys like Joe but they were Master's born boys and the third one was Master's wives helper boy. Despite whatever their jobs were all of the field hands hated them and called them names.

The house boys and gals just cleaned and cooked. Joe, Kate and the other hands cooked for Master and all of the slave workers. The born boys took care of all of Master's horses and polished his riding saddles. They were the plantation's blacksmiths and such.

Master's wife's helper boys were hated by all the slaves because they were around Master and his wife all the time; opening doors, helping Madam board her carriage, straddle her horse and carrying Madam's boxes and packages when she went shopping.

The helper boys were always given the best foods and dressed in the best clothing like white folks. They made sure Master's and Madam's boots and shoes were shinned and polished. Whenever there was a house party or guests were invited they were present to serve the guest.

The Madam came inside of the kitchen once or twice too often unannounced and would find Kate and Old Joe arm in arm. Madam believed they had been doing something the "Good Book", talks against, even though they didn't know how to read the good book or any other book. The Master's madam was a Christian lady and she certainly was not going to allow such carryin' on in her house. The madam would only laugh when she told the Master. He said, "If it keeps happening he would just have to use the broom on both of them." Joe and Kate overheard their Master saying this and they tried to stay hidden but they were constantly being caught.

5

Calm Before The Storm

Tornados come and go in these parts leaving their devastation for others to witness. Kate was an eye witness to the damage that one of the fiercest tornados left on many a victim.

Our new Master, Little Rob Henry was not the greatest master and he certainly wasn't the worst either. His sister had moved out West and had heard that her pa was ailing and she and her family had come to visit when he died.

One of his sons had died with the fever a few years before old man Rob Henry died. Mister Little Rob really didn't want to be tied down to a plantation; he wanted to be a rodeo rider.

Often times he would tell of how he could ride the horse no one else could ride. He was thrown more than a dozen times by big bulls, however there was a horse known around three

or four states that no one ever rode more than
a minute that he claimed to have ridden.

A rodeo had come to town and everyone had
come to see this "Tornado." The ring master
would show the stallion to the crowds every
night and some fellows in the crowds would take
sometimes a fatal chance to ride. The owner of
the show had pictures and a big poster that
had a twenty dollar pot for anybody that could
ride Tornado for more than three minutes. At
this time twenty dollars was a little more
than a month's pay.

A man named Big Hue had rode Tornado last
and was thrown, kicked and killed. The other
rodeo riders refused to even try and ride it.
After Big Hues death the animal hadn't been
ridden in over a year. Little Rob had placed
his bid and asked for a chance to try. Many
of the older riders laughed and said boy you
don't know what you getting yourself into.
Some of the riders chuckled and asked, "have
you ever rode before son?" "Sho I have," he
said.

"Well I tell you what," the wrangler said;
"this afternoon we got an old wild long horned
steer bull named Kicks and if you can ride old
Kicks' we just might make you a deal." That
afternoon Rob was loaded onto the back of Old
Kicks. There was a large rope tied around the
steers back with about three feet to hold on
to.

Rob had watched the other riders take the
left over rope and wrap it around their riding
hand and their free hand waving in the air. He
did as he seen everybody else do but he tied a
knot around his hand with the rope. The gate

was opened and the great bull lunged forward and began to kick and buck. Little Rob would have fell off, but his hand was tied to the rope and he had his feet locked under the big bull's belly. The ride seemed to last forever, but finally the cowboys came beside the big bull and pulled Rob off. The crowd roared, "ride-um cowboy, ride" as the clowns guided the bull back to the empty stall.

Rob was totally tuckered out, shok up, and sore all over as he limped out of the ring. He says to himself, well I guess I just lost my chance to ride Old Tornado. He heads for the stands and sees the wrangler who gave him his chance to ride the huge bull and there was a half ways smile on his face as he said, "that was a good ride son, go on over to the chuck wagon and draw your pay." He limped to the wagon and there was the ring Master and the owner. The owner said, "son you dun really pretty good, how many bulls you rode befo?" "Well to tell you the truth about it sir, it was my first." "Your first, but I thought you said you had rode before." "Yes, sir I did but never bulls it has always been horses."

"Well that's okay son, you did real good . . . in a ways too good." "I give anybody two dollars a minute for riding that bull." "Oh says Rob, so I guess I got two dollars coming hum?" "No, son you got eight dollars coming, you rode for four and a half minutes." "Oh thank you sir, Rob says after receiving his cash in silver! "And here's your other money son!" The man hands him ten dollars, in two five dollar gold pieces. "What's this for sir?" smiles Rob.

"Cause son you the youngest rider ever rode that bull for more than two minutes and I told my riders if anybody could ride for more than three minutes I would give-um ten dollars." "How old are you son?" "About sixteen come next fall or so."

The next day the stands were crowded with town folks and folks from everywhere and they all were just waiting to see who Old Tornado would throw, kick and kill next! The crowds came from the nearby villages, towns, counties, and some even come from nearby states. They all knew that on the final night they would see who was chosen to try and ride the unrideable horse.

The day was hot and dry and everybody seemed to have a bag of cotton candy in one hand and a jar or canteen of water in the other. People were enduring the clown acts and calf roping in order to see the final attraction of the day, the man that would try to ride Old Tornado.

The bronco riders were sent from their shots with terrible horses all would kick and snort the ground. One rider was thrown and drug around the ring before the clowns could stop and get the rider's mangled body untied. Finally, the last event of the day came and the ring master entered the center of the ring and says "and now ladies and gentlemen, boys and girls, the event you all have faithfully been waiting for 'Tornado', the black stallion."

Usually the crowds would only see a horse or any other animal after it was sent out of the shot with the rider. They brought Tornado out into the center of the ring. There were three cowboys that had ropes around his neck as he entered the arena the crowds all stood up and cheered. The kids all began to cheer and shout "that's him" . . . "Old Tornado the wild black stallion horse that ain't never been rode."

Tornado looked at the crowds as if he knew what they wanted from him, he reared up onto his massive hind legs and rears up for a few moments and pawed the air. He comes down snorted and pawed the ground. He angrily pulled at the ropes that were tied about his massive neck. He raged at the horses and cowboys that were trying to hold him fast. The crowd cheered one of the cowboys that was trying to control him was thrown from his horse. Tornado charged at the fallen rider, but the other ropes barely held fast; however he got close enough to kick and break the front leg of the fallen horse. The rider was injured, but was hurriedly removed out of the mad Tornado's path.

Tornado galloped around the circled arena as the cowboys rode along his side with their lariats trying to hold on. At first there were three men that had cast their lots so they could ride Old Tornado that afternoon. All three would be given their chance if one didn't ride at first.

Rob was the last to cast his lot. One of the lot casters was waiting with Rob, but suddenly decided he had business else where's after he had seen Tornado kick and break the leg of that horse. Apparently the other rider forgot what time to show-up, because he was no where's to be found. Rob was worriedly standing alone; suddenly a clown came forth and the wrangler said to Rob, "to get ready boy, looks like your numbers just about up."

A clown put a blinding handkerchief over the eyes of the unquilted stallion named Tornado. The clown waived his hand for Rob to come forward and let the crowds see him before he mounted the great stallion's back.

6
Tornado

Kate paused for a minute and smiled as she said she wasn't there to see the blessed event but they told her what happened. The story went something like this:

The crowds began to boo, as they saw the young boy. "Who's the boy?" "Boo, boo, boo" they all began to cry aloud and yell. "Who's the boy, boo, boo, boo." The stallion began to rear up on its hind legs again. The crowds began to roar again. Rob yelled out in anger, "what you talking about old man, I can do it." Another old fellow in the stands yelled . . . "the other riders are plum chicken yellow scared . . . at least let him try!"
   Tornado reared up again and pawed the air just like a prize fighter just before a fight who knows he's bigger and stronger

than his opponent and confident of a win. Bets were beginning to be made and ring out loud in the air. "I bet one dollar, he can't do it," some said twenty; one even said fifty. It was like David verses Goliath.

Rob was tall and slim looking and stood over six feet tall and weighed in at least a hundred and sixty or so pounds. His face was handsome but childish looking; he hadn't begun to scrape his peach fuzz yet.

The main wrangler jumped from the stands and entered the ring and said, "alright now, I've heard all of your sayings and I tell you what, let's see here I'll bet four to one that he does it and if any of you willing, put up or shut up; now's the time to speak up."

"I'll take two dollars of that bet," some said twenty-five and so on. "Ok" said the wrangler, "go give your money to the ticket man over yonda in the ticket betting booth." When he gonna try to ride . . . one of the women shouted out, "well let's be fair and square about this cause our money is at stake here; go on put that there horse in the shot good and proper like." "Yeah, yeah," the crowd shouted. The wrangler agreed, "All right then yawl we gotta be fair bout this here now ain't we; boys go on put Old Tornado in the shot good and proper like, just like the folks want." Old Tornado pulled and jerked so hard until the two riders were unable to force him into the shot good and proper like. Other riders came and lassoed him also and helped force him into the shot as he pawed the air and ground and snorted endlessly.

Everyone shouted "all right now alright . . . yeah . . . yeah . . . Tornado." All of the other riders came out rushing into the ring and got Rob, cheering him on as they all were laughing. An old cowboy told him to make sure he tied the rope good and tight. The crowds were cheering as Tornado was hauled to the shot. Tornado was kicking and snorting and tugging on the ropes around his neck. Rob climbed the fence and loaded himself on the back of Old Tornado. He tried to rear up, but there wasn't enough room.

An old rider watched Rob wrap the rope around his hand and told him to unwrap that rope and put on his gloves so his hand wouldn't rub sore and he told Rob that they was betting a lots of money on him" and if he lost, they was all gonna kill him and he kept laughing.

One rider said, "son when he starts to kick and buck, you just hold on and just say to yourself; I can do it, I can do it!" One of the men said softly as he was setting a straddle the fence, "if you get thrown before the time, play like you've been knocked unconscious, cause the crowds may sometimes feel sorry for you and award yea a little cash for your effort." The blindfold was removed from Tornados eyes. A woman in the stands yells out, "stop yawl! Stop, we might not

ought to do it—that there horse might
kill that there boy . . . I was here and
seen when he killed my brother, Old Hue
last year." She threw up both hands and
fainted. Another younger lady screams out
over everyone else's voices and says,
"something's wrong about that there horse
from 'Hell', his eyes ain't right; look
up close, they fire red and I ain't never
seen no red eyed horse before." All I
ever done seen was gray and brown eyed
horses; that horse is from hell I tell
you right now."

An old timer with a corn cob pipe in
his teeth growls out, "Oh! Hush gal, yawl
women folk ought to have stayed at home
with your young-uns, setting in a rocking
chair with your knitting and sewing all
cozy like all snuggled up close to a fire
in yea fire place good an proper like.
Us men folk don't care if his eyes were
blue, green, purple or even red like you
say, as a matter of fact we don't care if
he was bread with a rattle snake, goat,
jack ass, or old Lucifer himself; all we
want is to get this here ride started so
we can win our money back right men?"

At last, the ride got started. The
crowds yelled, "ride-um cowboy, ride."
Some were yelling, "come on Tornado, I
got my last dime bet on yea and I ain't
never seen you been rode yet, kick Tornado
kick, kick horse kick, go on, kick that
there boy off yea."

"Ride him son, ride cowboy ride," the
wranglers and the other cowboys shouted.

Tornado rears up and falls down, but Rob still held on. He ran into the side rails snorting and paing the ground. Tornado ran around the ring trying to press Rob's leg against the rails, but Rob hung on and held fast. Tornado had all four hoofs off the ground at once raging like a newly castrated bull; mad like he had done gone and seen red. He was in such a rage until his head tossed to and fro but Rob somehow still managed to hold on. The great horse continued to kick and he kicked and pawed the ground then ran into two of the barrels in the center of the arena.

The old lady that had passed out had inhaled smelling salts from another woman's purse and had awaken and was standing to her feet cheering "ride boy ride!" "I think he's gonna do it!" Despite Tornado's effort Rob was like a leach on a turtle's back. The turtle hates the rider, but can't do nothin about it. The great horse's effort was fierce but Rob had his feet hooked around his belly just like he had done to the great bull, Old Kicks and he couldn't and he wouldn't let go. There was blood dripping from the inside of the glove the old cowboy had given him to help save his hand. His riding hand was now numb despite the massive glove he wore. The knot was too tight to undo or unloosen. The great stallion that no man could ride seemed like he was about to be rode by a young boy. He was like a fish with the hook caught in its mouth and the man is trying to pull it in. The Almighty God had already given to mankind or boy-kind the dominion.

Tornado pawed, kicked and bucked until he couldn't kick no more; he began to prance and slowly began to trot around the ring as the crowds cheered. There was no need for the clowns or cowboys to drive him back into the stall. Rob had rode and broke Old Tornado.

He dismounted from Tornado's back and stood in the center of the ring. The crowds were cheering, "alright son, alright, that's alright." Some even said, "Although I lost my money son you did an outstanding job and it was well worth it." "Yeah boy you dun did it; I only wish my brother Hue could have been here and see it." A cow poke came up and handed Rob a bridle. Rob put the leather studded bridle over Tornados head and put the bit in his mouth and led him into the stall.

Everyone looked on and cheered as Tornado entered his stall and ran twice around his stall and stood in the center and reared up its massive weight and pawed the air and whinnied out loud! That was the largest bronco riding purse Mister Rob had ever won.

7

You Must Be Drunk

Kate was really beginning to warm up now. As she told the story of Rob's wedding day, she changed her voice each time she relayed the events of the day. She began by describing the day.

The day was warm and a summer rain had just fallen and all the dust was gone. There was a knock on the door and Rob hurried to open it. There stood an elderly fella, in his late fifties; all dressed up in his Sunday go to meetin' clothes.

"Come on inside," said Rob, "Man ya sho do look good in that there Prince Albert suit and string necktie."

"Why! thanks ya," his friend said. And ya don't look half bad yourself with those polished boots and shiny spurs."

"I got one of the boys out in the field to scrub and brush down Old Tag my riding horse and I'm ready to go.'

The friend said, "Now Rob ya know riding a horse to where we're going ain't good and proper like. Where we're going folk always leave their riding horses at home and take their fine buggies and carriages to show off."

Rob said, "Oh good night, now Clarence what we got to make such a fuss about; what we gonna ride and how we gonna get there, besides ya know good and well I don't own no buggy."

"I know said Clarence and that's why I got mine tied out front for you and me to go in."

"Well Clarence, I guess I'm as ready as I'll ever be.

They both got in the two horse drawn buggy and began down the road.

"How ya feeling Rob." He asked.

"I feel just fine but I think I plum don forgot something. Oh no, quick turnaround I recollect what it is that I done forgot."

Clarence pulled back on the reigns of the horses and stopped the carriage and asked, "What ya dun forgot man?"

Rob said, "my pistol, man my pistol."

Clarence whistles once to tell the horses to get-e-up and he smiled and said, "man ya don't take no dat blame gun where we're going and for what we're going to do.

The horses galloped down the steep road and they began to slow down as they got at the bottom of a narrow tall hill, as the horses strained and tugged up the hill it seemed to be almost too much for the horses to overcome.

Rob and his friend both got down from the carriage and they both lead the horses over the tall hill. The road began to plain out and they stopped the carriage and let the horses rest a spell. After about twenty minutes or so they both boarded the coach and continued their journey.

"We only got about another half mile to go before we get there."

"I know," said Rob shaking his dropped down head.

Clarence said, smiling, "Sure ya ain't forgot nothin else?"

"Nothin I can think of," said Rob, "not at the moment anyway but it still seems to be something I'm forgetting." Clarence looked over at Rob with a half grin on his face and said, "now Rob, I know ya don't really think I fell for that story back at your house about ya done forgot your pistol did ya?"

"Ya not trying to change your mind about where we're going are ya?"

"No, of course not" smiled Rob! Rob looked over at Clarence and said, "Let me see, inside of my coat pocket I got a little bottle of . . ."

Before he could say anything, Clarence said, "Now Rob ya know better than that, go on and put that stuff up."

"Rob said," All I want is just a little drink," he took him a swig.

Clarence said, "well boy I tell ya what, before I did what ya about to do I took me a drink too, so how about giving me a little drink to help me forget past times."

About a quarter of a mile from where they were going, there was a huge field of wild flowers. As they came near to it, Clarence said, "whoa" to the horses and puts on the brakes ties the reigns to the brake handle, and both men jump down and start towards the wild flowers. They both picked a bouquet. Rob said "ya know who I'm picking flowers for but who ya doing it for?" Clarence smiled and said, "My wife." "They sure smell sweet don't they?"

"Yea they sho do," said Rob. Clarence said, "Now Rob ya can't pick all colors like me boy, ya got to pick only white flowers for this type of occasion." Rob said, "but, but, but . . ."

"But nothin son, take it from me; I know about such things."

"Ok." And they got back in the carriage.

The horses slowed down their gallop as the small town came in view.

"Well," said Clarence, "I can see the bank."

"And I can see the saloon" said Rob.

Clarence said, "Yeah and look I can see the church," as he smiled and looked at Rob. "Let's go straight to the church now!"

"I don't think so, said Rob, let's go to the saloon first!"

"Now Rob," said Clarence.

"Oh Clarence, said Rob, ya know I was just joshing. But let's do stop for a second so I can have me one more last drink." "Now Rob, man ya know ya ought not to be going into God's house after drinking that stuff but go ahead and give me one last drink too."

They finished up the small bottle, wiped their mouths and threw the bottle into the bushes and continued down the road. As they drive through the familiar town; folks were walking and riding towards the town church and spoke to both men and women, some would say, "Hi Deacon Clarence I see ya got him, now don't ya let him get away, we can't wait to see this." Some elderly ladies even said Mister Rob, "I see ya finally headed in the right direction."

They got only about a couple of hundred yards away from the church and Rob saw an old girlfriend named Mollie and she was headed towards them and he told Clarence to hurry up the horses. Before he could say why, Mollie had seen Rob and she had begun to chunk stones at the horses and Rob and she was yelling, "ya low down, good for nothin free loading skunk, I was your girl at first and now ya dun gone and got another and you're an old drunk too." The horses hurried on past the angry woman. Clarence laughed and said, "I guess that was one of your well-wishers huh!" Rob said, ya know Clar-e-n-c-e after I's . . . I's . . . don . . . finished . . . [hiccup] . . . doing what . . . [hiccup] . . . I'm going to do . . . [hiccup] . . . this here day I'm . . . a . . . g-o-n-a . . . . s-t-o-p . . . . . [hic-cup] drinking that.there [hiccup] . . . s-t-u-f-f boy . . . I's . . . s-h-o .do. feel.go-ood . . .[hiccup] . . . don't . . . y-o-u . . . [hiccup]. Clarence . . . Clarence said, "Yea, I, sho do to Rob!". . . Clarence looks over at Rob and says "oh naw! b-o-y. y-o-u drunk! a-i-n-t ya?" [hiccup] . . . Rob say, [hiccup] . . . [hiccup] . . . "h-o-w can y-o-u . . . to-tell?" Clarence says, [hiccup] b-e-c-a-u-s-e you're hiccupping.

8

The Road to Amanda

Ms Kate continued to describe Rob's wedding day with all its splendor and it was a hoot.

The buggy pulled up to the tying rail; they both jumped down and hitched up the horses. Rob looked around and said "I don't see Amanda's buggy anywheres but I do see your wife Clarence." They both went to the water trough and got them a drink.

Clarence said, "We better wash our faces first boy before we go inside the church and sober up a bit."

They washed themselves and straightened up. They walked to the door and opened it. As the door opened, the parson stopped for a second as everyone turned around and saw who it was.

The parson looked and saw that it was Rob and he said, "Well praise the Lawd, Deacon Clarence ya did get him here on time as a matter of fact ya got him here way before time." The whole congregation burst out with 'Praise the

Lawd'. Some of the young folk began to giggle.
One of the elderly ladies said quietly, "now
ya young folk ain't nothin funny about what
this man is doing and is about to do, I just
wish my four sons would stop doing what they
doing and pattern their lives after his."

"An-a-ra" said the parson from the pulpit.
Some of the young and old folk sniggled out
loud and one little girl setting next to one of
her little girlfriends said, "It's sho gonna
rain today."

Clarence went to the second row from the
front and sat next to his wife and handed
her the flowers he had picked. She smiled and
said, "Thank ya darling, I love ya." He held
her hand and said, "yea and I love ya too
[hiccup]." Rob went toward the back but one of
the elders of the church went back and got him
to sit up closer to the front. As he walked
toward the front all eyes were on him. He sat
down on the first row in front of the pulpit
next to all four of the church's deacons.

The preacher said, "well Brother Rob, we're
all sho glad to see ya, ain't we yawl?" "Amen,"
the congregation said. "Before I, continue on
with this morning's sermon about '*The Evils of
Drinking*', would ya like to say anything to
the congregation brother Rob since we ain't
seen ya for so long?"

Rob stood up and said . . . [hiccup][hiccup]
"Well I's guess I'm." The preacher interrupts
and said "I'm sure you're just trying to say
yous glad to be here right, brother Rob?"

Rob still standing and said, "[hiccup] right
P-a-r-s-o-n . . . [he cup] . . . I, ain't been
here since my Ma-a-w.d-i-e-d . . . [hiccup]."

The parson says, "Well Mr. Rob seems like to me ya dun gone and got yourself a case of the hiccups ain't ya?"

Rob said, "yes I's, I's, I's sho have" and sat down. The parson said, "why don't ya go get yourself a drink so ya can get rid of those hiccups?".One of the deacons whispered into the ear of the other deacon sitting next to him, smells like to me he already done had one drink too many already, and that's why he's got the hiccups now. Rob answered the Parson and said, "yeah r-e-v-erend I,I, would l-i-k-e another d-r-i-n-k but deacon C-l-a-r-e-n-c-e and m-e d-u-n d-r-u-n-k it all u-p."

Clarence's wife turned his hand away and said, I thought I smelled that stuff but I never dreamed it was on ya." A small tear dripped down her chin; she frowned and softly said to him, "wait till ya get home, sucker." He smiles and says . . . [hiccup] . . . [hic—cup] . . . "hum."

The parson continued with his sermon and the saints were Amen-in' and praisin' the Lawd. The preacher was reared back whooping like a tall man during a hog calling contest

"We need to take all of the liquor and alcohol and pour it in the river." Rob was sitting there not saying a thing except to ask is anybody had seen Amanda Smithshoe? A little old lady was setting in the back of him and tapped him on the shoulder and asked him to be quiet as she continued on asking him when was the last time he was in church. He told her since his Maw died, why?" he says. She went on to say "young man don't ya know that you're supposed to be quiet when the preachers a preaching?

Rob asked, "Why's that, ain't everybody else yelling and hollowing and stuff. Why can't I? All I, want to know is if anybody seen my girl Amanda?"

"Well so, ya will hush up she's at home getting ready for this afternoon service.

This afternoon service, well I wondered why Deacon Clarence brought me here so quick. "Hey says Rob, look my hiccups dun gone! The sister says praise the Lord. Yes praise the Lord say Rob. Folks were shouting and crying and finally the parson asked if anybody wanted to give their life to the Lawd and he extended the invitation and says, "If anybody needs to come to the altar please come now." No one came but Rob says, "Well Deacon sense no one else will (standing up still holding the wildflowers in his hand that he had picked earlier and he says, "Preacher, "I do" Clarence stands up and says, not yet Son, not yet, as he tries to get Rob's attention to sit back down.

Rob got up and went to the front and took the preacher's hand. Everybody in the small church began to shout, but the young folks began to giggle. The little girl that had said before it going to rain today, said quietly to her mother sitting next to her, "The water gonna get muddy today." Her mother said, "Oh hush gal.

As Rob gave the parson his hand, the parson said, "Well thank the Lawd, Brother Rob it's been a long time comin' do ya want to be saved Brother Rob? Rob say, I, do. The church shouted Praise the Lawd! The parson asked,

Brother. Rob do ya want to be dipped in the water today? Again Rob said, "I do!" Deacon Clarence said out loud, "Rob, Rob, Rob not yet son, not yet, ya don't know what ya doing." The parson said, "now brother Clarence I don't believe ya saying what ya saying, if brother Rob wants to be dipped, I think we should go and dip him don't, ya folks?"

All the congregation shouted out with a hardy Amen! One of the deacons came up and taken him to the back and put a baptismal robe on him. The parson was about to ask was there anybody else that wanted to dipped when he was interrupted by a loud noise outside. The little girl leaned over and whispered to her mother, "ya see I told ya it's beginning to thunder . . ." "Oh! Hush gal, didn't I, tell ya?" the mother said.

The parson starts again to say does anybody else wanna be dipped. As he finished speaking ya could hear the wind blowing hard against the planks on the outside of the church. People began to quiet down as ya could hear the rain beginning to fall on the tin roof and the room became dark as the clouds covered the suns bright rays. People could hear the rain outside falling in buckets. The parson said quietly, "Someone go and close the door befo all the rain comes inside and floods the floors."

A sudden quietness came over and upon the entire church as the preacher said, "Lets all just sit down and be real quiet as the Lawd's work is going on outside and when the storm passes we will walk out yonder to the pond and dip our brother Rob." The little girl's mother leaned over to the lady sitting next to

her and said, "ya know what my little gal's
right again she always says when a plain out
rite sinner or drunk comes to church and don't
know what they're doing it always rain. After
fifty minutes or longer, the storm passed
over. As the storm was raging the church folk
were constantly in hard prayer for the new
converted soul.

One of the old elders raised up his head and
said, "Praise be to the Lawd, the storms dun
passed over so we can go and dip our new saved
brother." The little girl whispered to her ma,
"I don't think he's no sain't; not the way he
smells." "That man's still a sinner just like
me!" "Hush gal, didn't I tell ya . . ." Clarence
leaned to his wife's ear and said, "Honey he
just don't know what he's doing!" "Oh! Shut
up man, why ya saying that?" "I'll tell ya
later." She responds with, "Okay, hum."

Everyone headed to the back door of the
church with the parson holding on to Rob's
hand. Mother Smith began to sing a hymn. "Take
me to the water to be baptized". As they got
to the door and opened it the clouds were
just beginning to roll away and the sun had
not fully come out. The little path from the
church leading to the pond was soaked with
water from the rain and the mud had begun to
flow towards the pond.

As the congregation approached the pond it
could be noted that the banks were flooded
from the heavy down pour. The pond's bottom
usually was clear and sandy, but now it was
muddy from the silt and sand that had poured
in from the nearby banks. It was now nearly
impossible to see the bottom.

The sound of tree frogs and crickets'
squeaks were present and pot holes left from
the flooded water. One could see there were
fish trapped in the newly made pot holes and
they were trying to swim back into the main
stream but couldn't. Most of the folks were
now angry with the parson for wanting to dip
someone after the pond had swollen.

Their polished boots and buttoned down shoes
were now covered with mud and dirt from the
short walk, the old women were beginning to
complain about the mosquitoes swarming at their
necks, arms and bare skin as they scratched and
slapped themselves. The sand and horse flies
were beginning to be a nuisance and some folk
were beginning to say some of those little not
so Sunday school words under their breath.

The parson took Rob by the hand and said,
"I would like for one of my deacons to help me
take this fine brother out into the water."
Someone said out loud, "why not let Deacon
Clarence do it?" Clarence responded with,"
Well I'd love to but that water looks a bit
swift to me and if I lost my footing I might
get swept away and ya know I can't swim, why
don't we let your husband do it?"

The parson smiled and said, "Now, now everybody
it's OK! I really don't need any help; I can do
it by myself." He took Rob out into the brim
of the muddy water and Rob fell. As he slipped
another cloud came up in the sky as a small beam
of sunlight penetrated a corner of the cloud
and struck the top of the silt filled water.
Rob stood back on his feet shaking in fear. He
was raised to his feet by the Parson and tried
to go out into the deep water.

The song begun to get louder . . . "Take me to the water." The wind begun to start up again as Rob inched his way into the deeper water, and the water mysteriously became colder and colder than it had been ever before.

"Hurry on son hurry on," said the parson, "the devil is trying to stop this here dipping ain't he yawl? I can just feel it."

The clouds began to roll again the thunder was getting closer and closer. Tiny drops of rain were trickling on the pond's surface. Many of the congregation folk had become mad and were saying if he don't hurry up they was going back home because they didn't have parasols or a slicker to keep the rain off them and they didn't want to catch cold.

The poor Parson could see lightning strike a tree some distance off and knock it down. The feel of lightning was in the water as the Parson could feel the shock of the lightning hitting the water. He felt like it hit his elbow and he could feel the charge going way up his arm and into the tips of his fingers. The preacher was even becoming afraid. Large logs were floating by from the saw mill that was upstream from the church.

Parson Patterson looked up towards heaven and prayed to the Lawd for a sign. The little girl says, "ya see mama, I told ya he ain't gonna do nothin cause he don't know what he's doing and God ain't gonna let him get dipped just ya watch and see!"

"Child I hope ya wrong but I hope he do something cause I don't want to get wet." "Do ya still want to do it Brother Rob?" asked the Parson. "I do," replied Rob. Rob was standing still shivering to death from the ice cold water. Clarence shouts out loud to Rob, "no, boy no, I'm trying to tell ya, not yet." He shouted out, LAWD PLEASE GIVE THIS PO MAN A SIGN." Rob and the parson now have walked out about waist high in to the water but still not deep enough for Parson Patterson to dip him.

Small snowflakes lightly fell on the banks of the pond and rain drops fell on the surface of the pond the sun went in and out of the clouds. As Rob slowly inched his way into deeper water, there was a loud splash that came into the water as if a huge log had fallen in to the water.

As the parson coached Rob onward, he and Rob could see a couple of long eleven or twelve feet logs coming towards them floating under water.

As the logs came closer, not any of the congregation could see what the two cold and frighten men in the water could see. One of the logs peeped out of the water and they both seen that it wasn't logs but it was cotton mouth water moccasins and a couple of gators, as they spied them, the Parson said out loud for Rob and everyone to hear, "do ya think we should just change our minds about this and do it some other time?" Rob said, "Yes Lawd yes, I do!" The Parson said, "I do too." They all went back to the church. The little girl said, "see momma, I told ya." Mom says, "yeah I know ya told me gal ya dun told me."

They all went back and prepared for the evening service. Clarence took Rob to his house for dinner. As the two men drove up in their carriage, Parson Patterson had already beaten them there and was already in the house. Clarence and Rob entered the house.

Clarence greeted his wife with a little kiss on the face, "How ya doing Parson?" "Just fine," he said, "How's ya both doing now?" "Just fine," they both said together. "Dinner's ready," the house maid said, "Go wash up and come eat." After dinner as the Parson left he told everybody that he would see them all in a few hours. Everyone said okay.

Clarence's wife asked Rob if he wanted to take a nap before they went back to the evening service. "Yeah, yeah, I don't mind if I do," he said. They led him to a bedroom where he could lay down and rest a while.

As they left the room and went to a closed door room of their own, Springtime said, "Clarence, now sucker, what ya doing drinking before coming to church?" "Now, now, Springtime," said Clarence. "And what ya mean by telling Rob in church he didn't know what he was doing and that junk ya were yelling out about not now?"

"Oh (a he he ya) see Springtime, honey, Rob don't know nothin about church or church going on." "Ya know what he's supposed to do today, don't ya?" "Sure I do," replied his wife. Clarence laughed, "(he he he he). "What so funny?" says Springtime. "What ya just said!" "What ya mean what I just said?" The words "I do". "Ya see Rob ain't been in the church so long until he dun plum forgot what to say anymore in church." "What ya talking about Clarence?"

"Ya see gal Rob asked me before he came this morning what all he was supposed to say and I told him any time the Parson asked him a question all he had to do is say, 'I do'." Springtime said, "Well, ya mean when the Parson asked who wanted to be saved that's why he said I do?" "That's right," said Clarence, "and when he asked if he wanted to be dipped; he said 'I do' again." Springtime said, "So that's why he kept saying "I do" to everything the Parson said." "I was wondering why when we was eating and everyone was stuffed and the Parson asked who would like to eat anything else—Rob said 'I do'!" (a he he he), "Yep that's it."

Rob was awakened and they all boarded the carriage. Rob still had his flowers that had begun to wither and the petals had begun to fall. They entered the church grounds and saw all of the church folks already there waiting. The little girls all pretty in their white dresses and hanging ribbon tied bonnets. People were in their best suits and stove pipe hats and chain watches showing on their vests.

Outside of the church there was about four tables already fixed with white table clothes and several baskets of food sitting on their centers. On the center table there was a cake with a punch bowl surrounded by silver cups and a ladle ready to be dipped. The smell of good home fried chicken and freshly baked bread was in the air and people were all standing around waiting in participation. As Rob entered the door, a great awe was heard over the entire foreground of the church. Clarence's wife went up to the front of the church and sat down.

Rob looked straight ahead and saw Amanda standing almost center of the preach pulpit. She seemed to have a handkerchief to her eyes weeping in fear that he was not coming. As she saw him she began to perk up with a smile. She stood in the same place that the communion table had been earlier.

Her dress was arrayed in all sorts of fancy needle work and beads around her neck and a crown like the angles wear in the picture books. Her face was lovely as Rob looked on even though it was veiled.

Her father was there also proudly standing next to her all dressed up in his Prince Albert tails as Rob walked toward Amanda; his heart began to rush and pound as he saw and felt his destiny only a few yards in front of him. Clarence never left him but stayed close to his side. Clarence says soft to him, "Now son now's the time for ya to go and take her hand and give her flowers you been faithfully carrying all day."

He went forward to the altar and handed her his flowers with a big proud smile and look on his face. Her mother, sitting on the third row wiped her eyes as he then takes her hand. "Who gives this woman to be this man's wife?" "I do," replied her father and sat down. All of the words and vows are said and done.

All at once, the Parson looked sternly into the face of Rob and said, "Now Mr. Little Rob Henry, do ya take Amanda to be your lawfully wedded wife?"

Clarence whispered to Rob, "Now say it son." Rob looked at Amanda and pulled back her veil and said, "I do!" Then he kissed her. The rest is history!

9

Name Him Joeson

Kate once again began to reminisce about the days and times she had with the love of her life, Old Joe. As she rocked back and forth, she told this story

Before coming to the big house, Old Joe learned where the eightsitter little house was. The mess house was up wind from that spot. Old Joe found out in a hurry not to be late for mess call. He once came late to chow because he was working a field alone. He had to wash all the pots, pans and dishes, but it had a good side because he got to eat all the leftovers he wanted.

When Old Joe arrived at the big house and first saw Kate he began to smile. Kate's job was to cook, clean and take care of the Master's house. Old Joe first learned how to cook and later he learned how to clean, sweep, scrub the floors and such in the house. Old Joe had fallen in love with you know who, even before he had come to the big house. He made sure he learned the job fast. He had also learned the way to Kate's little shack after dark when he thought no one was looking.

Joe looked at Kate and asked her who her beau was. She responded by asking him (with a frown on her face) what was it to him? With a grin on his face, he told her that a pretty fine looking young gal like her had to have a man somewhere. She asked him why he was thinkin like that. He said cause anybody could see that she was in a family way. She tried to deny it and insisted that her belly wasn't in no way fat.

He told her it wasn't her belly but her neck. It was a lot darker than the rest of her body and her face was lookin swollen but her face was just as petty and as bright as the sun when it first comes up.

He told her that he had seen other women folk in the family way before and they all had what she had before their children came. He told her she even had big veins on the side of her neck and they were all puffed up and jumping hard and fast with blood.

Kate began to frown and dropped her head and soft sobs came from her mouth. She cried softly, "Oh, my lord, my lord, so that's why I didn't do this month what I've been doing every month before, my Lord, My Lord." Respectfully Joe put his strong arms around the broken hearted woman and confessed to her that he was sorry for saying what he said.

He tried to loosen his embrace, but his grip had totally overcome her. Her blood had begun to boil and her breasts were rapidly pounding as the tall strong black man returned his grip about her. She just simply couldn't take it anymore and she put her arms around the tall and strong man and just held him back and just sighed.

She looked up at him with pounding heart and closed eyes and she let her lips taste the sweet nectar of his lips. After holding him closer to her soft breast as she laid her tender head upon his strong pounding chest and after a few more lip touching and deep breaths and such they finally spoke. She told him she didn't have no beau and if she was in a family way she didn't know herself. Joe simply suggested they better get headed back up to the big house before Master came looking for them.

He couldn't resist her anymore and asked if he could be her beau and come calling on her. She tried to play hard to get by shaking her head back and forth, teasing him with an "I'll consider it," she finally said.

Joe still wanted to know how she got in a family way cause he wanted to rub his head in the dirt, and hog mud and hang him.

Kate still wouldn't name the one who got her in a family way but she did confess that she had considered him some and decided she just might let him be her beau. She urged him back to the big house to fix the master's rocker arm.

They both climbed down the ladder and headed towards the barn door, but before Kate could open the door Joe reached out and held her hand one last time and embraced her and planted a hard smack on her lips.

Joe sat on the porch steps and began repairing the rocker arm as Kate returned back to the kitchen and peeped out of the window smiling and waving her fingers as Joe glimpsed over his shoulders.

Amanda came out of the front door and saw Joe at work and complimented him on his fancy work. She asked where he learned to do such fancy work. Joe told her he had learned it from his last master, Master Smith, and that he actually learned how to make all sorts of pretty store bought furniture.

Amanda asked if he meant Jamison Smith the store owner. Joe confirmed what she asked. Amanda told Joe that the last time she was in that store she saw one of the prettiest bed and bed dressers she had ever seen. She asked Joe if he thought he could make one like it for her.

Joe smiled and told her he sure could and even more. Amanda asked Joe if he would whittle something for her. Joe said he'd be mighty proud to do something for her. He made her extra happy when he told her he could even cut her out one of the beds like she had seen in Jamison Smith's store.

About two days later, Amanda recalls to Mister Rob the event that had happened on the front steps. Amanda began to tell Rob that Old Joe told her the biggest lie. Rob asked what she was talking about. She told Rob that Joe had told her he could make store bought furniture. Rob told her that all of them don't tell big lies like she thinks.

Amanda told Rob she wanted him to give Old Joe a good whipping because he said he could make her a bed just like the one she saw and wanted at Jamison's store. Rob replied that she was the one who needed the whipping and not that man out yonder. Rob recalled who she was yapping bout.

He said that the one she was talking about must be one of the new slaves that he just put out in the rows and fields. He asked if she could remember which one he was. Amanda admitted that she didn't know his name.

Amanda asked Kate to bring her another piece of fried chicken. Kate put a chicken leg on her plate and whispered to her that the boy she was talking about was Joe and there wasn't but one Joe out yonder in the field.

Rob sort of remembered getting several boys from Jamison's store. He said Jamison had told him that some of them did know how to make stuff out of wood. It seemed to him that all he got out of that bunch was fights. He had been considering getting rid of all of them and getting some non-fighters.

Amanda told him she didn't care what he did with the rest of them as long as he kept Joe. She wanted Joe to stay and make her some of that fine store bought furniture and stuff like she had seen in Jamison's store. Rob said he wasn't keeping no dat-blamed slaves here just for making her dat-blamed furniture. Amanda began to sob and accuse Rob of being mean to her. She threatened to go back home and tell her daddy how Rob done broke his favorite child's heart again.

He said, "Amanda honey you don't have to go and do all that again and cause hard feelings between me and ya Pa again. Please honey not

that." He said, "There's got to be something
we can do to please you and keep ya happy;
don't cry baby doll."

He asked Kate if she could use some help in
the kitchen. He recalled her saying that she
could use a man sometimes to help with the
heavy work in the house and such. Kate spoke up
saying that she didn't recollect that. Amanda
looked at Kate again and winks her eye.

Kate began to help Amanda with her cause
saying that she's so tired now days and how
she couldn't stand and that she sure did need
some help. Rob finally agreed that it sounded
mighty fine after all. He told Kate to go fetch
Joe so they could get the boy started.

Joe began his new job as cook and housekeeper.
Shortly after his arrival at the big house,
Kate couldn't scrub the floors anymore because
she was too big in her belly. Joe kept the
house for her and he had learned how to make
Master's meals.

Poor Kate often had to take little naps
during the day and every morning she would be
sick. Often times she would pass out when she
got too close to heat or fire. Joe still took
care of all of the work to be done in the big
house and up into the wee hours of the night
he would do his promised whittling.

As lady luck would have it Joe would always
be there if and when Kate got sick or dizzy.
He never did try to approach her as a man would
his wife but his love for her was immeasurable.
At times the Master's misses would catch him
with his arms wrapped tightly around her.

The Master had threatened to use the broom on the both of them if they continued to misbehave.

One morning about four months later after hearing what had been said, Joe saw Kate holding her stomach and rubbing her side. Joe asked her what was wrong. She told him she could feel a kick and she knew it was about time. Joe was concerned that if Kate didn't have a beau when the baby was born, the Master would only let her wean it and then he was going to sell it. He felt that she wanted to keep the baby. She had tears welling up in her big hazel brown eyes and they began to fall down her cheeks as she confessed that he was right, she wanted to keep her baby.

With the baby coming, Old Joe professed his love for Kate. Kate then let down her guard and told Joe that she loved him too. She slowly reached over and held his hand and she turned loose of the back of the rocker and reached up and kissed him on his face.

She thanked him for everything he did for her. She confessed that he was the only man in her entire life that she ever cared for and loved except her pa and little brother Eli who were both dead now (she continued to cry).

As Kate silently stood there talking, she noticed Old Joe reaching over and getting the floor sweeping broom which he laid on the bottom rail of the chair. He said he wanted to ask her something. He asked her if she would be his woman and his wife.

Kate dropped her head in a great moment of silence and held her stomach and looked up at him with sad, but grateful eyes.

She said to him that if she said yes, he knew no good and well that what was in my belly wasn't his.

He told her that she was wrong because he loved everything about her from the first time he laid eyes on her and that meant whatever was inside her belly too.

She told him that he could sure say the sweetest things and that he really knew how to steal a gal's heart. She told him she did have to say that she admired his kind of love, if it was for real, but she just can't say yes to being his woman, not yet anyhow. She told him to go ahead and move the broom before she started bawling her eyes out and change her mind and say yes.

He demanded to know why. He asked if he had done or said something that bothered her. He felt she owed him some kind of explanation. She told him that he hadn't said or done nothin and that he was as good as he could be and sometimes better.

She told him that she thought that he may love her some or even a tiny bit he just might even love her a whole bunch but she wondered if he was just feeling sorry for her. Joe responded by telling her he was not feeling sorry or any pity for her. He said he had been in love with her since he first seen her. He promised her that somehow she would see for herself just how much he loved her then she would be his woman and his wife.

As they both were headed back to the kitchen, they can hear Master's footsteps coming through the front door. Master greeted them with a hello and go fetch supper. Kate then yelled,

"OH . . . OH . . . OH, it's kicking." She grabbed her stomach and sides and said she thought it was time. She was calling on the Lord and yelling that something was wrong inside her. She told them to go get Big Momma cause she was the best midwife in those parts.

Kate screamed . . . "Oh Lord, Oh Lord, I can fill it coming. Somebody do something; Lord, help me; Lord, Lord, Lord, please."

Big Momma came running in from the field. She wiped the sweat from her brow, because of the hard run to get there. She was old and had helped to deliver many a child into this world. Her braids were white as a new snow on the hillsides, her hands were withered and torn from many years of toil in the rows, her face black and wrinkled from the heat of too many summer suns but because she's a lady she's still thought to be beautiful.

As Big Momma entered the door, Amanda just happened to walk up and she could hear Kate's cries coming from inside the house and she wanted to know what was wrong and what was going on in the house. Big Momma told her that Kate's time had come. Amanda went inside to help.

Big Momma told them to hurry and go fetch some boiling hot water and a pan of hog lard and some rags because the baby was almost there. She told Amanda to help hold Kate's foot and told Master he could help hold the other foot.

She asked Joe if he could hold both of Kate's hands. The hard push had begun and everyone was instructed to hold her tight. Suddenly Big Momma told Kate to stop pushin' because something was wrong. The child had turned sideways. She told the Master that she needed a doctor really bad or she just might die with that child in her like that.

The doctor was too far to go get. Amanda yelled, "What you mean, the doctor ain't no more than a few miles away?" Rob told her he didn't' care if the doctor was up stairs, he wasn't spending his hard earned money for no slave child to be delivered.

Joe told Rob if he wouldn't do it then he would. Joe turned loose of Kate's hand and went to fetch a horse to ride to get Doc Waters. Amanda told Rob that if the child is born dead he could just start looking for himself another wife.

Rob dropped his head and told Joe to go ahead and fetch the doctor and if asked who's ailing don't tell him a slave cause he might just take his own time coming. Rob said if ya tell the Doc it was him that's ailing then he'd come in a real hurry. Big Momma said, "No Joe, just hold your ground a moment." She told Kate to just lay quiet and still a moment cause she had seen Doc Waters do this more times than you can shake a stick at. She couldn't wait for the doctor now, the child was at the door ready to be born into this unfriendly world.

Big Momma asked Master to just turn his head for a while she talked to the good Lawd for help. Amanda told Rob to close his eyes and pray for once in his life for someone else besides himself. Big Momma quietly prayed and Amanda said a prayer with her.

She had to go inside Kate to turn the child back around. She told Kate that she would try not to hurt her bad. She told Joe, to come swap places with her. She asked Amanda if she could hold both hands at once. Amanda said, "Oh, yes I can, go on and do what you got to do.

Kate could be heard screaming, "Oh, Oh, Lord, I'm dying this baby gonna kill me; Oh, Lawd have mercy." Amanda held her hands and began to sing a little song . . . "Come by here my Lord, come by here, cause somebody needs you Lord, please come by here." Big Momma wept a little as they all can hear the sweet and mournful song that pleaded for God's help.

Big Momma told Kate to take a couple of deep breaths and that she was gonna fix things. She asked the Lord to guide her hand in Kate. She told Kate just to hold on a little bit longer. She told her just to hold as still as she could and told the others to hold her tight.

Big Momma told Kate to cry Jesus as loud as she could. She told her to cry Jesus cause he would turn her baby back straight. Big Momma removed her hands from inside of her and told her to cry Jesus. Everyone in the room was sweating, but they all were shouting Lord Jesus.

Even old hard hearted Rob was saying, Lord for this once please have mercy. Just then Master Rob began to smile and said thank you Lord because even then he could see the head coming. Momma said go ahead child and shout Jesus and give Big Momma a few more hard pushes.

Kate screamed, "Oh Lord I'm dying," as she gave a final push. The baby had come all the way out. Kate fell back in the bed. Big Momma told Amanda to take the baby because Kate had fainted and wasn't breathing any more.

Joe began to cry, "No, lord no." He ran to the kitchen and got a glass of cold water and threw it in her face. She laid there for a second or two and then she began to shake some and cough. Old Joe leaned over to her and held her head and told her she had scared him there for a moment as he held her head and softly kissed her cheek.

He told her that no matter what happened, he loved her. Amanda put her hand on Kate's face and said she loved her too and she did real well. She smiled and told her that she had been a bit worried for a moment, they all thought they had lost her.

Kate was too weak to raise up in the bed, so she just laid there and cried and said, "thank you Lord Jesus, thank you, I sure do thank you Lord Jesus." "I might not be able to keep it but I sure do thank you anyhow and Lord the baby's alive." The child was a male, however, during the delivery one of his legs seemed to be slightly twisted. After a few days of Kate's rubbing and patting, the leg corrected itself.

Rob began to talk and tell Kate that she had done mighty fine. He told her that cause she didn't have no beau, he had to sell the baby after he got weaned. Old Joe looked at Master Rob and asked Master Henry what he was talking about.

Rob repeated himself and said that Kate didn't have no beau and she couldn't keep the baby, he had to sell it. Big Momma wanted to know what Kate was going to call him. She explained that usually a new born boy child takes the name after his Pa. Everyone began to look at one another as if to say who's the pa?

Kate looked up with her child in her arms and with great big tears in both of her eyes and said she wasn't gonna tell. Amanda said she thought she had known all along but just kept quiet (she looked at Old Joe and smiled). Joe agreed with her and said that the child was his.

Rob looked a little puzzled but Old Joe stayed with the story. He's my child sir, he said. Rob then said that if he was Joe's son that he would have to be named after him. Rob told him that he didn't know how good that had made him feel.

Amanda questioned Rob about why he was so glad. She said from the look on his face maybe he thought it was someone else's. He just told her that she was imagining things again.

Kate said that she sure did want the baby named after his pa. Amanda held Kate's frail, small black hand and told Kate she could name him whatever she wanted to.

Kate began to cry and said thanks. She thanked them all for helping her with the birth. Tears flowed down her face as she tried again to speak. She said he was the son of Joe so she wanted to name him Joeson.

Amanda still held her hand and repeated the child's name. Rob said he guessed he had to take back what he said about selling the child.

Amanda told Big Momma to get some of your stuff so she could stay up at the big house until Kate got to feeling a bit better. Big Momma said okay and that she would tell the rest of the folks in the rows bout Kate's new son.

Amanda said that when Kate got through ailing she was gonna make her and Old Joe jump the broom. Rob giggled at the talk of them jumping the broom. Kate was puzzled. Rob told her if Joe was her beau and the pa of her child, they ought to get hitched so she could be his woman good and proper.

Joe held his peace. Kate looked at Master Henry hard and deep in his horse gray eyes and said he was right then she turned her face away from him and pretended to fall asleep but cried in her heart.

Big Momma left the house to tell the good news to the folk out in the fields, but she did have to tell them the way the child was turned in the womb before the delivery and what she had to do before the delivery. Kate may never have any more children.

Parson Nails came over from Longstar Church in town for supper one Sunday afternoon and before he left Amanda asked him if he would be good and kind like and wed Kate and Joe. He agreed to perform the ceremony but without knowing they both were slaves. After he had realized they were only slave servants he refused to do the vows because he said all blacks were not Gods folks, they were the children of the devil and they all were just here on earth to be servants for all of the good righteous and saved white folks.

Rob was out of town when this happened. Even though he wasn't a church goer like his wife, he slipped out and got another good preacher from another county. He was one of those good Baptist, hell fire and brimstone preaching preachers, his name was Rev. Yonkato Trees.

He gladly did the ceremony and ate plenty of fried chicken, collard greens, turnip roots, cornbread, apple pie and good cold apple cider. At first he wasn't going to do it but after Rob had tempted him with a little money and promised he would feed him, his wife and his nine children, he was persuaded to do it.

Despite the fact that Rev. Yonkato had performed the ceremony, no slaves were ever considered to be legally married because they wasn't given the right to citizenship and they couldn't own any type of property. All they could do was jump over a broom handle or a wooden tree stump. Joe and Kate chose the broom, they held hands and were good and properly pronounced man and wife.

Amanda was very joyful for them both because she claimed to be a bible believer.

She had a dress made for Kate at Jamison's store. Old Joe had to take a bath and put on a clean change of clothes from Jamison's also. Master Rob even let a few folk out in the fields and rows come watch and after the preacher and his family, wife and nine children had eaten and left, he pulled the cork on a jug and insisted they both have a swig.

At first Kate wasn't very happy being married until the misses insisted that Master Henry built a little four room cabin for Kate, Old Joe and their new born baby. Her sadness soon vanished away!

After the assembling of their new house, Rob brought Kate and Old Joe over a jug to sip. Kate made her first meal in her new house with her new man and their new baby.

10

Coon Hunting

Now this is one of the funniest stories
that I have ever heard and Kate tells it
beautifully.

Kate and her beau were coming along just fine
with the house cleaning and meal preparations.
It has been over three years now since Joeson
had been born. He was always in the way; in
and out of the house while his Ma and Pa were
at work. At times one could say he got in the
ways too much. Ms. Amanda didn't seem to care
very much for the little child being in the
way all the time.

She would often yell and scream when he did
little childish things and more than once she
made remarks that she hoped she never would
have to care for no children. The child's
parents pretended not to mind what she did
or said to their son, but deep down in their
hearts they were hurt.

They knew there was nothin they could do
about the problem. They tried their best to
keep the child out of her way.

Master Henry seemed to adore the child and
always brought gifts and such to his parents
for him. Once he went for a ride into town and
returned back and stepped down from his horse
and picked up little Joeson. He asked him how
he was and told him that he got him a hat just
like his. He told him if anybody asked him
where he got it, just tell them your pa got it
for ya. He put Joeson down and he went back to
his playing.

A bit later in the day Joeson was back in
the house playing and running in front of
Amanda and he turned over a piece of furniture
and she yelled out for him to slow down in her
house. The small child whimpered and answered
his Master's wife and ran and held close to
his ma's dress and she held him. Master Henry
heard the commotion and asked why was she
hounding so much for? She told him why.

He responded roughly with her and said, "If
she acted that harsh with that child he'd hate
to see how she'd act with a child of her own."
She responded with a slammed door.

Rob stood there at the bottom of the staircase
shaking his head and saying, "Lawd, Lawd what
I done gone and said wrong now?" He headed
upstairs and tried to make up with her. When
he entered the bedroom and they began to talk,
she said she didn't rightly know why but, she
just didn't like that child no matter how hard
she tried. Rob told her if she wanted he'd
sell the entire family.

She said she really didn't hate the child she was just envious of his folks because they had no child of their own. Rob held her and said, "Yeah, Manda I know honey, but ya know I still love ya don't ya; and I ain't gonna stop loving ya if we don't ever have any young-ans." He kissed her and as he headed for the door, he said, "Ya know Amanda honey, why don't ya for try to pretend he's ya real son?" She told him that she wanted them to have our own child. Rob only replied to Amanda that he owned him and that made him his son and she was his wife and that made Joeson her son too and he walked out the door.

Amanda thought to herself 'that man Lawd that man, you know I love him even though I know he don't proclaim to practice the good book, he's trying to make me think he's Abraham and another woman done gone and had a child for us. For the next weeks and months she tried as hard as one would expect to get along and accept the child but she was still at odds with him.

Fall had arrived and it was time to sell off many of the older cattle. Rob planned a cattle drive and followed along with his drivers. Amanda always stayed behind to make ends meet. Late one afternoon after supper, Amanda had eased back for a spell in the swing on the front porch. Swinging in front of her were a few slave children kicking up their heels and playing in her front view. As the children were playing she was startled by out bursts of cries and screams coming from Joeson. "Ma, ma, ma, my eye, my eye." Amanda ran from her swing to see what the commotion was all about and she grabbed the child as he continued to say, "ma, ma, ma my eye." She tried to calm the child down as he cried, "get it out, get it out." "Get what out, son? what happened?", she shouted in fear.

"My eye, my eye." She picked him up and ran inside with him and his ma and pa said, "Oh! What's wrong?" Amanda said, "it's his eye, I think he's got something caught in it." "Kate go light me a candle, so I can have me a good look and get whatever's in it out." She removed a few small grains of sand from his left eye. Joeson put his arms around her neck and held her tightly. She smiled and said, "Now, now it's okay! Child don't cry it's gonna be alright." He finally calmed down and she said, "Now turn loose and go on over to ya ma," but he still held on. She tried to break his grip but he still held on.

Finally she began to laugh and give in to his little hugs and she softly said, "Now Joeson, son why won't ya turn me loose, do ya think I'm ya ma?" He answered and said, "Yeah, mama Manda I love ya." Amanda's feelings were turned inside out and she began to hold and hug him back and said, "Yeah child and I love you too, now you go on and turn me loose before I tan your hide and go on to your ma and pa."

When the child and his parents were turned in for the night, they were having a quiet talk. "Well looks like things beginning ta look up some for Joeson, just when we dun thought Ms. Amanda would never take a liking ta hem." "I's sho is glad ain't you honey?" "Yes I is." A few weeks later as they both began to doze off a soft knock came on their cabin door. "Who is

it?" asked Joe. "It's me, Ms. Amanda!" They
both went to the door and let her in. "What's
wrong ma'am?" I asked. "Oh, nothin's wrong, I
just came by ta ask a favor of ya." "What's
that ma'am?" "Well you see Rob's gonna be gone
for da next few days and nights and ta tell
ya da truth about it I, don't rightly like
staying alone and I need somebody ta stay da
night with me, if-an ya don't mind."

Kate spoke up and said, "If you don't mind,
we don't mind Ms. Amanda and I's be dressed in
just a few and will be right up ta ya house."
"Well Kate, I thank ya for da thought but I,
didn't really have you in mind!" "Well, I
said, I hope ya didn't mean my man Joe," with
a confused look, cause that ain't gonna look
proper like ma'am." "Oh no, she said, Kate
I didn't mean you or Joe, I really meant ya
little boy, Joeson", as she smiled. "Joeson,
you sho ya mean Joeson, our little boy?" "Why
sho I'd love ta have ya son Joeson come lay
next ta me, so I won't feel so lonely while my
man's gone."

"Sho Ms. Amanda I recon so. I'll go fetch
hem up and wrap some covers round hem so he
won't catch cold and Joe can carry hems for's
ya." "Oh, no, that's alright yawl I'll carry
him myself."

Joeson spent a few nights with Amanda until
Rob returned from the cattle drive. In her
heart she had begun to care for the little
child, but she tried not to show it in front
of his parents, so much. Now when he got in
the way she only laughed and said, "Now Joeson
you know better," as she rubbed her fingers
through his raggedy crow black hair; she looked

gamefully into his big bright, shiny horse gray eyes.

More time has passed and he was about twelve years old and both the Henrys' just loved him. When Master went to the fields, he always took the child with him but he never allowed him to work the fields like the other slaves. He always seemed to favor this child, but he would let him at times work with his parents at the big house. Joeson would at times call Master Rob pa and Ms. Amanda ma. His Master's wife constantly insisted that he would sleep in their house.

In the early spring of his twelfth birthday one of the mayor horses had folded and Amanda presented him with the young pony. She would also go out and purchase good clothing for him and take him on buggy rides. Many of the other slaves were jealous and envious of him. She and her husband were guilty of treating this child's parents special. Because of the favor the parents had achieved, through their God's grace, the other slaves were fed and clothed better.

The other ladies in town would only smile when they saw the child and missy on the same wagon. Once Master Henry and his wife were on a neighbor's ranch and the child was with them. Because the child was black and considered as any other slave; he wasn't allowed to enter the man's house, therefore he waited outside. As he waited, he began to wonder on the man's farm and saw an apple orchard. He had entered into it and began to eat on one of the delicious fruits. Four of the rancher's white workers saw him and they began to shout bad remarks at him and one had even caught him and began to beat him.

Amanda heard his cries and ran to the door to see what was going on. "Hey you, yeah you," she lashed out, "put that boy down and you leave him alone that's my slave." The man only laughed and continued to beat Joeson with a stick. Amanda called for Rob and as she screamed, one of the workers had grabbed her by the arm and had begun shaking her. Rob came running to the door. He yelled at the workers asking them what they thought they were doing. The man that had hold of Amanda turned her loose but the other one that had Joeson still held on to him and said they had caught Joeson stealing apples and all they were doing was trying to teach him some manners.

Rob told him to let loose of the boy or else go for their hog's foot. The worker pulled his pistol and got off one shot into the air, but he never knew where it hit because Rob had put two shots into him before he ever drew. One hole was square center of his neck and the other had parted his shoulder blades as he fell dead to the ground.

The other worker slowly drew his gun and threw it to the ground and said to Rob that he won this time but that they was gonna see who would win the next time. The ranch owner saw what had happened and he told Rob not to worry he had seen it all and he would get some of the men to go bury that dead swine trash and the rest of the three no counts were told to go draw their pay an high tale it off his ranch and don't ever come back!

As Rob, Amanda, and the child headed back to
their own plantation, Master Rob told Amanda
that maybe he should stay up a spell and watch
because he didn't rightly trust that riff raff
back there at old man Hats' ranch that he
claimed to be running off his ranch. For the
next few nights, Master Rob Henry got a few of
his hired workers to stay up and watch to see
if anything went wrong; however, luckily for
the next few days and nights all went well.

Amanda went on about her regular store buying
and Master Rob Henry did his crop tending.
Late that Fall just before harvest time, Old
Man Hats' came out to Rob's plantation wanting
to buy a string of horses and Rob saw with him
the other three gun slingers Hats pretended
to have run off his plantation. Rob made a
sell for at least a dozen horses. Hats seemed
to be real pleased with the deal him and Rob
made with the purchase of the animals. He said
thanks to Rob for the sell before he left and
shok hands with him.

He told him that he would be seeing him again
real soon, maybe sooner than he thought. Rob
smiled and said okay. The gun slingers also
smiled and told Rob what a nice place he had
and they were glad they knew where he lived
and that they may visit sometimes unexpectedly
like. As the riders left they passed by where
Joeson was riding his pony. One of the men
fired his gun into the air and spooked the
young horse and they all rode off into a cloud
of dust.

After supper for the next few days Master Rob
seemed to be a bit edgy because he remembered
the remarks that old man Hats and the gun

slingers had made concerning seeing them unexpectedly sooner than he thought. He kept his guns close and he had his workers alerted with their eyes peeled. Mid-week had come and gone twice and the edgy feeling had left and was forgotten.

Three weeks later, as Rob rode his horse across one of his fields; it had become terribly hot and dusty. Rob's' nostrils was praying for a little rain, as his shadow stood directly under him and his horse. About high noon Rob headed slowly back to the house for some of Kate's baked biscuits and ham meat.

There seemed to be a stench in the air but what he couldn't seem to figure out where it was coming from. He glimpsed across the horizon and noticed smoke coming from the south pasture and he could see Joeson running toward his and yelling something. He rushed his horse towards the smoke and Joeson and met him yelling Master, Master, Master, Grey Riders, Grey Riders. Rob said, "Where?" with fear in his voice. Joeson said they were at the house pa and down at the barn, Grey Riders" (Grey Riders meant hooded riders). Rob told the boy to jump on the back of his horse and show him and to hold on tight. He told some of the field folks to go run and tell my white men folk.

He rode toward the house and could see the Grey Riders leaving and going to his left. He told Joeson to get down from his horse and head back to the house and try to help chase the riders. He could see his white men folk in the distance now helping in the chase. It seemed to be about twenty or so Grey Riders.

Seven or more of them had just been cut down
by Henrys helper's gun fire. There were four
more in Rob's rifle range but he missed all
of them. He did get one in his left leg and
he fell from his horse, but one of the riders
returned back and put him on his horse and
they got away. Angrily, Rob returned back to
his house from the chase and found out that
one of the hooded riders had got caught and he
was asked where he was from, he said old man
Hats' plantation.

Rob snatched and removed his hood and asked
him before he hung him, why they did what they
did. He told him that a white man named Rob
Henry had shot and killed another white man
because he had caught him beating one of his
slaves for stealing apples.

Over half of Rob's south fields were burned
and one of his barns was burned to the ground
and nine of his best horses and three milk
cows and two slaves died from the flames.
For the next few days or so Rob was trying to
recover as much as possible of his barn and
rebuild it.

Rob decided to take a few of his men with
him and make a friendly little visit out at
Hats' Ranch. Hats' house servants greeted him
at the house. Mrs. Hats welcomed them all in
and asked them to have a seat as she had them
all a drink made. Rob told Mrs. Hats that he
had a barn burn down to the ground and over
half of his south pasture destroyed by Grey
Riders a few days back.

Mrs. Hats said she was so sorry to hear that
and asked him if he knew who any of them were.
He told her that as a matter of facts, he sure

did. She again said that she was sorry to hear that and said if there was anything she could do to help, just let her know. Rob thanked her and asked if her husband was around. She said yes, but he was all laid up now. He said what she meant about him being laid up

Mrs. Hats told him that a few of the boys said they were going coon hunting. She said he had told her that about three or four men got shot and about eight or so even got killed during the hunt. She said she told him to never do that again because she didn't like coons that much no ways for him to get killed over. Rob asked her if he told her that just to be sure. She confirmed it and asked Rob why he asked.

He asked her what her husband seemed to be ailing from now. She just said, "Lawd, Lawd, Mr. Henry didn't ya hear, everyone else in town knew." She thought he was coming to see how he was getting along. She said, "He got shot too on the hunt; in his left leg. Rob asked when she said that happened. She replied, "Few days back, why?" Rob said, "Well I was just wondering can I see him now?"

She said that he didn't feel good and the doctor said he needed to rest a spell and be real quiet like and not let nothin get him upset so much so he can start mending some before he started taking company again, and that he was getting old now. Rob asked how old her husband was. "If the good Lawd's willing next summer he'll be seventy-eight years old." She asked Rob how old he thought she was. Rob told her she was a fine looking lady and he'd say around forty something years old. She said he sure knew how to make an old lady feel good because she was nearly eighty four years old. She told him that she and her man had been for pretty near fifty four years and that they had twelve kids; nine gals and three sons.

She shared with him that one of her sons didn't care a darn for hunting that much, but her other two did seem to care a whole heap for it.

One of them was quite fond of going coon hunting with his pa, but the poor thing got killed trying to coon hunt that was one reason she wished his pa would quit. She said that if he got killed as old as she was now she didn't know what she'd do without him. Her youngest son got shot three or four times and he just gave it up.

She said she wished that her older son Ned had quit before he got killed. Her oldest daughter just pressed her pa to death to take her coon hunting with him; he took her along to see once and she came back and said it was just too much for her and she never did ask again.

Rob looked at her with a half grin on his face and said to his men that it was time to get going. He told Mrs. Hats that he was very sorry her man dun got himself shot trying to coon hunt. He asked her to tell him what happened out at his plantation and tell him he knew who those Grey Riders were and next time he wouldn't just wound, he'd shot to kill. She agreed to tell him and asked if there was anything else. Rob said nope but he sure got something he'd like for her to ask him, not for him but for her to ask him for herself.

Mrs. Hats asked what that would be. Rob said to ask him, "What type of guns were those coons carrying that shot him."

For the next two years there was no more serious trouble at Rob's place until one night at the town's church meeting Amanda mentioned that all store owners would donate small pieces of candy for the slave children for Christmas and they all second it and all the store owners did follow through with the idea and said praise da Lawd. The day before Christmas all six of Master Henry's smoke houses mysteriously burned to the ground.

11
Sisters

Kate recalled when she and Claire really saw each other for what they thought was the first time.

Every so often the slave masters would let their slaves go and visit the plantation owners on the other side to let them help friends gather their crops.

Kate's Master had loaned her out to Master Bird for a few days. Kate was the Master's favorite cook and house gal, however his neighbor Bird came over one day and asked Master Henry could he borrow a slave or two to help gather his crops.

Master Henry had asked Kate if she knew of any slaves that might want to go. Most of them didn't want to go because they had enough work to do in their own fields.

"Well could I's go Master, I's would likes ta go out of this house fo a spell and sees some different folk sometimes."

The Master asked, *"But Kate, who's gonna keep da house and cook while you gone Gal, if I was ta let ya go?"*

"Well Master let me see here, my old man Joe and my son Joeson could handle it until I's dun comes back. Please Master cans I go? Please Sir?"

Master Henry finally gave in and said,

"Well ok Kate ya can go, I guess, but if ya old man and ya son don't do a good job at cooking and such I'll send and have ya fetched (he smiles)!"

Kate smiled and said;

"Oh thank ya, thank ya Master and when cans I's go Master?" He told her Maybe da day after tomorrow.

Two days later Kate and several of Rob's slaves were carried by wagon to Bird's plantation and dropped off. They all were put to work gathering. Kate was put out into the fields, pickin' cotton. The fields were crowded with numerous slaves. Fall was at the heels of the plantation owners and if old man Jack Frost hits before the crops were gathered, all would be lost.

Ms. Kate is cat napping so we'll tell this story together. Slaves could be seen in the wheat fields gleaning and in the corn fields shucking and binding sheaves. The slaves were from several nearby plantations who were aiding in the harvest. The air was perfumed with the smell of ripened grapes, musket dimes, apples and honey suckle. Nature had predicted a hard winter was on the way.

The caterpillars' fur was long on its backs. The wild deer, buffalo, antelopes and other critters had long coats of fur down their backs too. The coves of ducks and black birds were seen in the skies flying southward earlier than before. All the creatures; squirrels, woodpeckers, ants, turkeys, chickens, wild bores and beavers were preparing for the winter.

While the slaves were working the fields they would commune with one another. Kate and Claire met each other out in the fields on the first day.

"How ya doing there?"

"I's just fine (says the strange lady) how ya?"

"I's doing fairly well."

"My name's Claire, what's yo-ans?"

"Mines Kate, please ta meets ya. How long ya been here?"

"Ta long" (smiled Claire) What's ya name again?"

"Kate, and what's you's again?"

"Claire."

The slaves were emptying many of their drag sacks onto burlap sheets and hoping for the dinner bell to ring. The day had begun with many dark rain filled looking clouds over head. Cotton fields had no cold days to a slave. The pain of a bent over back with fingers pulling the cotton from the bows and packing the sack as heavy as one could carry kept the slaves soul warm.

A slave never noticed rocks and roots tearing into the flesh of a bare foot for fear of falling behind and being seen by a row master and being whipped. Work was hard and tiresome and only a gourd of water and a morsel of bread would put the pain at ease.

The dinner bell finally rang. They all got their food and went to their own eating place. Kate was new in this field so she followed Claire who sat down under a tree to eat and wait for the water wagon to come by and get a gourd full of drinking water. While they were eating they began to talk.Claire said, *"Now Kate honey you be careful not ta talk ta loud cause Master don't like fo us ta talk ta much whiles us is taking vittals. Hem says it makes us lazy; so talk softly child. Who yor Master, Kate?"*

"Master Rob Henry."

"Who he and where he comes from?"

"Hem says hems folks came clear cross da big waters in England some where's by a big boat thing called a ship. Old man Tom Henry was Master Henry's Pa. Old man Tom was a bad slave Master. All of hems slaves just hated hems. Hem made all of hems slaves work from sun up ta sun down."

"Most plantation and slave owners would wake up and begin working after da rooster dun crowed but old man Tom would beat and whip any slave that would let the chickens wake up befo dem. Hem dun had three boys and a tall long legged gal. Mr. Tom, Mr. Tim, Mr. Rob and Mae Tae was their names. Hem dun treated dem just like hem dun treated da rest of us slaves, sometimes worst."

"*Hem made all of da slaves calls hems Master Tom. Hems "chillen" had ta calls hem Master too. Once hems little old ugly long legged gal Mae Tae called hem Pa when some other plantation owners and other white folk was over taking dinner and hem dun beat that po gal half ta death after dem dun gone. Her already was ugly as the devil but hem just made that there po child mo uglier.*

"*Once a slave or two called hem pa out in the fields and all hems dun was laugh and smile. Don't any of us understands hem or really knows why hem do the things hem does. Honey hem twas real strange. We's ain't never seen the Mammy of non of hems chillen. Rumor had it that hems ain't never been married.*"

"*Hem had an older brother that would comes over sometimes and dem would both get drunk together. Some of da plow boys say dem dun over heard dem talking bout dem's past an dem dun told how dem Ma and Pa had done got killed by dem own slaves, honey.*

"*Why did dem slaves do such a thang as dat Kate honey? Well, child ya see dem says dem Ma an Pa was whipping a slave grandma causing her dun gone and took one of dems chickens and was boiling it in her stew pot an her hadn't asked fo it. When da other slaves took notice dem dun got real mad and dem was trying ta stop um but dem ended up having ta kill both of Master's ma and pa.*"

"*Child you don't say and what else dun happened after dem dun gone and dun dat?*"

"*Dem says dat all of dem slaves' men dun laid with and dun had hems ma befo dem dun killed* hers' to child. All of us slaves believe cause what dun gone and happened ta Masters folks was whys' Master Tom just hated all us slaves and that's why hems so hard and mean ta us and always beating on us. Us were trying ta do whatever Master told us ta do in a hurry."

"Once when dem both twas full of dem liquor and twas drunk, Master Tom twas going on how at night hem would sneak an lay with a slave gal. Both the brothers laughed and told da same thang. All of Tom's chillen was mixed; Rob was hems only real white son. When Master Tom was in hems prime, how old hem was I's don't rightly knows but hems said hems dun meet a young, sun corn yellow haired woman at one of dem bars, one night an hem dun fell in loves with her an a few days later hem an her dun gone an got hitched. Shortly afterward would her dun got "knocked" an Masters fust son was born. Yeah honey that's how my Master dun comes into dis here world."

"While Old man Tom was still in hems liquor hems was still laughing and telling how after Little Rob was bone hem had cames home one day and caught hems wife in hems house in hems bed with another man . . . hem says da man was hems best friend."

"I tell ya what child, white folk a mess ain't they?"

"Yeah dem sho is honey yeah dem sho is!

"Child I's tell ya what."

"What's dat Claire?"

"I's sho wouldn't want no friend like dat."

"Me neither Claire."

"Hems dun says hems dun killed da man and afterward hem says hems dun beat hems wife near half ta death. Her was so scared of hems until her never tells nobody not, nobody bout dat there killing. Hems dun had dat po gal so scared and hems warns hers' if ans hers ever told anybody; Hem dun swore hems would kill her too."

"Child ya don't say and what else dat low down scoundrel dun let slip out child."

"Let me tell ya what else honey, ya ain't heard da half of it."

"Hurry up and tells me the rest Kate cause we got ta start back ta work in a few!"

"Lawd, Lawd, child, hems says dat one day hems just comes back home from work in da afternoon and her was just gone and hems ain't seen her since."

"Old man Tom took hems son Little Tom ta town an dun bought hems a small farm. Hems later bought hems some slaves and started hems a plantation. Hems slaves worked da fields an dem dun raised peanuts, cotton and cone. I's still can recollect when I's twas fust comes ta Master Henry's plantation. Child I was nothin but a little gal, bout nine crops time old I recon. My ma an pa died of somethin dem called scarlet fever. I's didn't knows dat much den child when I' fust got there but I's do recollect dat I's was scared ta death."

"I's ain't never seen nobody wit nothin like dat but I's sho nuff dun seen folks with da pox. Dem dun looked like an old dog with da mange's. Sores, all times scratching an stank, Lawd, Lawd, do day stank!"

"*Scarlet Fever what's dat honey?*"

"*Child it's a mess I's dun seen a whole heap of white folk with it; dem be running at both ends. Ya don't say child. Yeah Claire an dem be plum out of dem heads, dem be hot one moment an shaking da other, screaming an talking all out of dems head. Claire interrupts and says, ya don't say child, some folks dat knew my folks once told me dat my ma an pa dun died from dat same thang ya been talking bout.*"

"*I's can recollect I's once had a sister and brother but don't knows what dun happened ta my older sister. We's was separated and we was sold and took ta different Masters when us was real young.*"

"*Ya don't say child cause that's da same thing dat dun happened ta me. I's dun prayed ta da good Lawd, dat one day maybe I could sees dem again. I's been making it all by myself.*"

"*Ya knows what I's been told da same thing bout my folks.*"

"*Tis you thinking what I's thinking; child could us be sisters?*"

"*Ya knows what; us sho could be hum. We both do talk alike some.*"

"*Dos ya no's ya Ma and Pas names?*"

"*I's sho do . . . Mas name was Sally and Pas name was Eli.*"

"*What you dun said child as she (smiled).*"

"*I's dun said my Pas name was Eli and my Mas name was Sally.*"

"*Do ya member ya brothers name?*"

"*I sho do, hems name was Eli too, just like Pas.*"

"*Oh, no, it can't be.*"

"*It can't be what?*" (Kate frowns)

"*Oh my God, Lawd, my Lawd you dun gone an answered my prayer* (sob)."

"*What you talking bout Claire?*"

Claire begins to hug and put her arms around Kate and softly said,

"*Kate, honey, yous my sista.*"

"*Your sista, how do ya know dat Claire and what on earth ya talking bout child?*"

"*I's just knows Kate; I's just knows! Yous bout da same age she ought ta be and yous da same color she was da last time I's dun seen her.*"

"*Ya might be right but there's only one ways us can be for sho.*"

"*What's dat?*"

"*I's can recollect dat my sister had a fish of some sorts of a birth mark on her left leg.*"

Claire burst out in tears as she reached down and pulled up the left side of her skirt and pointed to something that appeared to be a trout fish out of the water.

Now even Kate began to weep and laugh at the same time as she shok her head to and fro.

"*Wait a few here now Claire if you really is my sista I's can recollect when us was separated, I's was took by myself and my sister and my younger brother was sent together and if yous truly my sista where's our little brother Beau and whatever dun become of hem?*"

"*You see child Master don't let us women folk and da men folk work together ta much cause hems says us gets our eyes off of da work and on one another.*"

She smiled and said, "*Kate, honey, me and Beau is still together child, hems over out yonder in da corn fields gathering and shucking corn.*"

"*Both sisters said together "There is a God! Now us both knows fa sho there is a God.*"

Claire and Kate softly cried together.

"*God does answer prayer, yes hems does, yes hem does!*"

They both slowly and silently stood up and look at one another over and set back down side by side on the ground.

Earlier Kate was setting sideways telling her prolonged story as she seldom would look up at the stranger's face. Claire before now was looking downward and wishing Kate would hurry and finish her tiresome tale.

Broken hearted, separated, torn apart and without hope and in slavery, but now tears of joy reunited these sisters as they sat side by side; Kate on the left and Claire on the right.

Kate had her right arm and hand around the neck of Claire and Claire had her left arm and hand around Kate's back and her right hand reached to hold and clasp her sister's other hand and just hold her.

It was cloudy and rain was in the air when this morning had first begun, but now the sun had come out and a hand seemed to have come from nowhere and swept the dark clouds away. Both heads were hung down in a prayer of thanksgiving and both were weeping. As the wind blew through the trees, one could hear out in the far distance an echo saying:

My sister, Lawd, Lawd, my sister! My Sister, My Sister! You may believe what you want, either by chance, luck, or call it fate or does God really answer prayer? Something has brought da sisters together again!

12

Handsome

Talk about handsome; I never laid eyes on such a handsome face befo in these parts.

The wind began to blow and the smell of dust surrounded the women's faces. Everyone was trying to hurry and finish up the long row of cotton they were on but the wind was determined to prevent them. One of the elderly ladies looked up and began to shout, "A storm is comin'. Look way over yonder she said, the clouds tis building up and da skies is beginnin' ta set real low . . ."

The thunder had begun to clap and lightning was flashing way out in the distance. A wagon pulled up and a voice yelled out, "Come get on yawl and let's head for the barn." The women folk scrambled to the wagon as tiny rain drops began to kick up the dust in the dry fields. Rain was now beginning to pour in buckets.

The black mules that pulled the wagon were kicking because of the sound of the thunder

clapping its powerful voice. All of those that
couldn't get aboard the wagon were now running
towards the barn. As the harvesters all headed
toward the barn they could see other wagons
heading in the same direction. The plantation
was huge and it had many barns in which to
store the different crops of harvest.

Claire hurried over to me and asked was I
okay? I told her, Sho I's okay, just a little
scared and my heart was jumpin' real quick
like that's all! I asked why we came inside.
An elderly man overheard me and laughed as
he mocked me sayin', "Why we's come inside?"
"Cause it's raining . . . can't ya see fo ya
self gal?" he laughed. I told him that at
Master Henry's plantation if it started to
rain, all we did was to keep on working. He
said that the rain helped to cool us off.

That man said, well you ain't on Henry's
Plantation now, you on Master Bird's Plantation.
He said I needed to get away from dat old slave
driver cause he ain't no good anyhow. He said
everybody had heard how he had chillen by all
his slave women folk. He went on to say that
Master Bird was a good Master. He said if the
slaves get wet and come down sick then they
couldn't work and make money for him.

Kate's story continued with the barn door
swinging open and a man coming inside to tell
everybody the rain had passed over and it was
time for everybody to get back out to the
fields. The man was a small short white man
with dusty brown hair and blue eyes. He wore a
blackish brown buck skin hat and an old dingy
looking gray shirt with blue looking overalls.
His boots would appear to have been Army boots

but they were the wrong color. His face was rather handsome despite the noticeable scar just below his chin line. The scar seemed to have been a burn mark.

I held back my smile in fear that someone would notice me. He's rather handsome I thought to myself. The man spoke with a rather soft and easy voice. "Before we go back to the fields, is any of ya hungry, thirsty or overly tired?" he asked.

I thought to myself, who tis this handsome white man and I ain't never heard such a kind voice coming from no white man, not one of them. Some of the slaves said they was a little hungry.

The man softly said, "Go on up to the kitchen room and get yourself a little somethin' ta eat and drink right quick like then head back to the fields." Claire ran over to me and told me to stop gawking so much and do what the man don said.

The man looked over at me and asked if I don came from over from the Henry Plantation. I said yes. He asked me did I eat before I came over.

I told him I had not because Master Henry told me to eat where I was gonna work at. The man told Eli, make sure that I ate till my belly was full before I went back to work.

"Yes sir," Eli replied. Two other slave women boarded the wagon. Eli drove up to the kitchen house. Claire didn't know I was going for food and water so she returned back to the fields.

On the path to the kitchen house I made sure I sat next to Eli. I said to him, "so

your name tis Eli hum?" "Yes mam it sho tis!"
I sat there staring at him as the other two
ladies tried to cover their laughs, because
of my starring. After arriving at the kitchen
I hesitated to get down from the wagon and I
intentionally held him up. "Can I's put my
arms round ya Eli?" I said. He began to smile
and said "Why I recon so; I's don't sees why
not if ya really want ta mam!" "Eli ya knows
I's still loves ya don't ya?"

Eli says, "Ya do, I's don't knows who you
tis, and why ya loves me anyhow, Look lady
I's married and I's don got nine chilrean." I
said, "look here long lost brother of mine I's
don't care if-ans ya got a hundred chilean I's
still love ya," as I kissed his cheek again
and again.

"Now wait a second here gal," as he holds
Kate back, "what ya talking about; is you
crazy?" "What ya mean what I's talking about,
man don't ya knows I's ya sister?" "My sister
what da world ya talking about woman I's ant
got now, nor dos I's ever got any sister, I
twas bone an raised on this here plantation
and my ma and pa both dead and I'm dems only
child."

"But Claire don told me that her and my
brother Eli were both here on this here
plantation." Eli begins to laugh! "What's so,
funny Eli, ya mean ta tell me ya ain't really
my brother?" "Befo I's can answer ya child can
I's has another big hug froms ya child?" "Well
I recon so, but why?"

"Honey take a good look at me, I's as old as
dirt, my hair don turned the color of ripened
cotton and my choppers in my mouth don all but

fell out and child face it as pretty as ya tis
as much as I'd like ta be, us don't favor no
where's; don't ya knows what ya own kin looks
like child?" "No I's don't cause I's ain't
seen him in years!" "Go on and go look in that
there window over yonder child and ya can sees
him."

I said "which one old man?" Eli says, "gal
ya must be blind, it ain't but three of them
in da winda." I said, "but I's still don't
no's which ones my brother." Eli says, "what
color is you gal?" I puts my hands on my hips,
pokes out my chest and said, "I's black just
like you tis why?" Eli says, "what color tis
dem there three men tis?" "Naw I's ain't blind
bro, but at times I's can't sees dat good so's
I's gona take me another look see I's recon."

"Let's sees here now, two off dem tis white
and da others black like you and me." So,
which one's ya brother missie?" "Oh ya thinks
ya funny, huh old baldy, I's knows I's ain't
white and I's don't want ta be, and I's ain't
stupid ya knows darn well I's black, befo ya
asked such a stupid question, but I's can till
ya one thing fa sho I's ain't even half as
black as ya tis."

"I's tell ya sometin else, my choppers
ain't falling out my mouth like a Halloween
pumpkin like yaws tis!" Eli couldn't help from
laughing. He said, "Now Kate ya don gone and
don got fretted ain't ya?" I told him that I
wasn't mad yet but he was about to make me
fret. "And what makes ya think dat with ya old
bold headed black self." He said, "Now, now
Kate I's didn't means ya any harm."

"What tis da matter gal?" My bottom lip was poked out, both cheeks were full of wind, my left hand was balled up, my feet were scratching the ground and both of my eyes were rolling to and fro, wrinkles had formed over my forehead and drops of sweat had began to fall from the tip of my nose. I shouted right out loud, "I's canst stands fa folks ta poke fun at mes ya old bald headed thing; I's got good and well sense enough to know that there black boy in the middle ought ta be my brother, I's recon."

The other women folk that came with me were looking out of the winder laughing and grinning and I finally realized that I was being disrespectful to the old man. I threw both hands to my mouth in total embarrassment, and said, "Oh mister I's so sorry, I's thought . . ." Eli just smiled and said, "It's okay, I understand but it sho twas nice ta once again have a young lovely thing like ya putting her arms around me," as he laughed, "go on and go sees ya brother now, gal."

I went inside of the kitchen house and the other ladies that had been looking outside were still smiling as I came in. I was trying to hide my embarrassment and tried to explain to the other women folk but they only laughed and explained that they knew and for me to go on and go see my real brother.

I walked into the kitchen and stood behind my brother wanting to call out to him and embrace him but I couldn't because I was scared stiff. One of the ladies in the room saw me standing there speechless and frozen and called out for me and said, "turn around Eli and see who's standing behind ya." The young man had a dark olive complexion with heavy muscles and even though he was setting down I realized he was tall and handsome. He quickly responded to the lady that called out to him and put down his fork and slides his plate a little to the left of him and turned around.

I was still frozen with joy and both hands lifted high up in the air. He made his turn and saw me and stood to his feet in amazement and total disbelief. The six foot three man trembled and breathed deeply and screamed to the top of his voice, "Kate, Kate, Kate, Lawd Kate, my sister Kate!"

Eli was big and as strong as any young bull. He was the head leader and spokesman for the plantation slaves. Many a row master had lashed his back with their whips but he never changed his speech. The lash made many cry out, but he always managed to hold his peace. He had seen and been through many a crop time harvest, hungry, tired, discouraged, and faint, but nothin ever drew tears.

Once he had been thrown and kicked by a wild stallion and had three ribs broken but he never let his master know he was even hurt. He and my sister had been sold and traded off four times but he always withstood and bore the pain.

Eli and I embraced and the entire room became silent for a moment. In the stillness and silence one might have been able to hear the sound of water falling from the surrounding slave's eyes. Old man Eli could barely refrain from wiping his own eyes. The six feet three inches tall man that had been beaten, whipped, thrown, kicked, sold and traded and even hung upside down and wouldn't cry, is now crying! The rains that bore up Noah's Ark were deep and Joseph and Jacobs reuniting tears were long but Eli and my tears were deeper, longer and they were soul disturbing.

After we both had calmed down for a moment or two I asked him how he knew who I was. He told me, he had been told of me from the other slaves and they had said I looked like his other sister Claire. He told me I was a pretty gal! He looked around and spoke to the other slaves and said, "Ain't my older sister pretty yawl?" All of the slaves in the room began to laugh and say, 'She sho tis, she sho tis! I asked him if I could call him Bro like I used to. "Sho ya can sis ya can call me whatever ya like!" "Bro I's so glad ta sees ya and yous so handsome. I's always don wanted ta knows and sees da both of yous and specially Claire." "You wont nothin but a little bitty thing when I's don last seent yous!" "Us got ta get back ta work now sis but us gonna talk again real soon honey child." "Honey, honey, honey, I's just can't hardly wait." They both hugged and kissed each other on the face and headed back to work.

13

Runaway

Kate and Joe were being questioned over and over again about somebody's whereabouts.

"Now where did ya say she's at Kate and Joe?"

"She's upstairs in the guest chamber Ma'am."

"My Lord, my Lord I know our Ma's worried to death about her."

"And ya say she done told ya what Kate?"

I told Ms. Amanda that Joe had answered the knock on the door and I went to see who it was. The woman had asked us if this was the Henry Plantation and we told her yes ma'am. She told us she was your sister and she had come to stay.

Ms. Amanda wanted to know why we didn't tell them when they first got home instead of waiting until they had finished eating super. We told Master Henry that after she came she ate first and she said for us not to tell you

103

until you finished eating first and she and Joeson had already made friends.

Rob asked Amanda if she wanted him to go upstairs and fetch their little runaway guest and have her come downstairs or did she want to do it.

She reminded Rob that she had told him that her sister was headed there the day before when they got that message from her mother that her sister had run away from home. Ms. Amanda said her would go get her but Rob needed to promise, to go easy on her because she was only a child.

He said to her that ain't no sixteen year old woman no girl and most folks would almost call her an old maid at that age. He went on to say that he had seen women folk younger than her and they were married and already had a house full of young-ins and grandchildren. She told him to hush his mouth about her sister and to stop laughin'. She went upstairs to fetch her sister.

Amanda woke her sister up with a hug around the neck and asked her to come downstairs to the table. Jennifer said she would be right down after she fixed up her face a bit. She fixed up a bit and came down to the eating table and sat.

Rob looked at her and smiled and she returned the gesture. She looked almost identical to Amanda. Her hair was mixed fire chimney red and with blondish brown highlights and her curls were like Amanda's. Both sisters had similar eyes and facial features with fair complexions; however Amanda was more mature looking. Both of the women were very beautiful!

Mister Rob was very fond of his wife's only sister and considered her as his own. Amanda started right in on Jennifer wanting to know what happened between her and their Ma back at the ranch. Ms Jennifer asked her if she could get a great big hug from Rob Henry before she got to answerin' that question. He gladly gave her that hug. He told her that we had all been scared half to death about her. He told her he was gonna have to let her ma know where she was.

She said, yes, she knew. With a smile on his face he asked her why didn't she fix up your face some first like you told Manda she was gonna do before she came down? She put her hands on her hips and asked him what he was trying to say. He hugged her and they both began to laugh. He told her that she was just as pretty as ever; just like a rose in the Spring time.

She ran away because there was no more schools where she lived and she wanted to continue on learnin'. Her mother had promised her she would send her to her sister's so she could attend another one of the fancy schools but it had been over two years since her mother made that promise.

Her mother always promised to send her in the next few months but never did. Rob and Amanda sent a post and a cable gram telling her mother that Jennifer was safe.

Where Jennifer had come from there was much talk about slaves and slavery but she had never seen or been in contact with any. In the beginning she was a bit afraid of them because she had only seen other whites in her entire

life and the first time she saw a black person
was a frightful thing for her.

In only a short while she began to accept
the concept but she would privately question
her sister about the things they had been
taught from the good book concerning loving
all folks no matter what. She had taken a
liking to Joeson from day one. She once told
Amanda and Master Henry she kind of thought
Joeson was handsome. Rob only smiled and said
I think you need spectacles too!

Jennifer started school three weeks after
her arrival. Her mother offered to help pay
for her schooling but Rob and Amanda refused
her money and told their ma it wasn't any
trouble because they both really enjoyed her
presence.

As Jennifer returned back from school every
afternoon she would at times go visit Joe and
Kate's small cabin. She was studying to become
a nurse. Joeson would question her about what
a nurse was? She told him that it was caring
for the sick and ailing just like a doctor.
He told her that he sure wished he could say
what he was thinking but he wasn't nothin but
a slave. Jennifer kept trying to get it out of
him. We finally told Miss Jennifer what our
son was trying to tell her was that we ain't
never gonna be nothin but slaves cause we ain't
free. Joe said, that if they was to ever get
caught trying to read or learn letters that
Master might kill them or he might beat or
sell them. Joeson told Miss Jennifer that it
was true that Master Henry was mighty good to
them but that they were still scared to death
to get caught trying to better themselves.

Jennifer responded to the problem and said she understood. She said she knew more than she did when she first came once she got to know the folks down here and started going to school.

Joeson asked Miss Jennifer what she was talking about. She told him that she knew and understood that the slave folks wanted to learn how to read and write their letters like any other folks. She had sense enough to know that we wanted to be free. She said if it was her she would too. Jennifer reached over and hugged me and kissed me on my cheek and patted me on the back and she embraced Old Joe and patted him on his back and gave him a little peck on his forehead.

Joeson saw this and he stood up and he smiled and shok his head up and down in approval and all he could say was well, well, well. She looked at Joeson and hugged him and told Joeson she was going to make him her little brother and she was going to figure out a way to teach him his letters and how to write. She said she might even show him how to talk good and proper like if the good Lawd's willing. She also said she might even try teach him how to escape from this awful thing we call slavery!

Never before had there ever been any hope of any slave learning to read and write. The upcoming weekend Jennifer found herself at our cabin. She closed the door and very quietly began reading to us. Joe and I paid it no never mind, but Joeson took a real interest in how to read. Jennifer knew her safety was at stake, therefore she told Joeson to keep secret that she had taught him to read and write.

He finally understood the proper use of the English language but he knew to keep it secret around other white folks and continue to use words such as we's, I's and us's. Jennifer had begun to read the good book to us and she tried to get us to understand the concept of faith.

Most slaves already knew how to pray in their hearts because if any white person would ever hear them praying out loud they would be beaten or killed.

A few other slaves were allowed to hear the readings and began to learn their letters also. The selected few were all sworn to silence. Jennifer showed and taught many private and secret things only to Joeson. The two had begun to get a sparkle in their eyes for each other but they didn't want anyone to notice. Amanda caught the look more than once and jokingly asked Jennifer about it.

Jennifer denied the look but Amanda wasn't easily fooled. Amanda could see that the two did care for each other but she keep it hush, hush. Blood was thicker than water.

One of the slave women forgot and was talking in the fields about a man dying on a tree for everybody's wrong doing. A white row master overheard her saying this and asked her where had she heard such nonsense from and why was she telling the other slaves that junk? She realized what she had done but only told the row master she had heard it from one of her former slave masters.

She was whipped with many stripes and warned never to be caught with that in her mouth any more. Many of the slaves knew how to pray and those on Rob's plantation were no exception. There were only a handful that secretly knew their letters and how to read some. Jennifer had told them it was no big thing not to know how to read and write, cause many of the whites had the same problems. Jennifer once told the slave family the story of a white fellow she had met during her schooling in town and she soon figured out he couldn't read. The story went something like this:

Well James I tell you what it does seem like you and I have known each other for quite a spell now. I can quickly recollect the fust times I dun gone and asked ya would ya give me da honor to come calling on yaw.

Can you recollect the first time I saw you James, you had done gone and got all busted up by some cowboy at the saloon. Sho . . . did and I twas brought over ta ya hospital ta get my head fixed up. Da fust times I dun saw yous, I's twas waking up and ya was putting dem wet patches on my arms and cold rags on my head and saying something like, you alright mister, is ya alright, can ya say something? I dun woke up and dun seen yous pretty white face and da white room and ta white dress ya had on and after seeing all that white I thought I dun died and dun gone ta heaven.

Oh now James you ain't trying to flatter me now are you? Of course not now gal a pretty little thing like you, but I do think you do look just like one of them there angels things just like the ones ya sees in da picture books and my heart just goes thump-d-thump and just flies away ever times I dun seent ya!

Oh! James now . . . Oh! Now you dun gone and made me blush . . . you don't really think that now do you? Of course I do! Waiter, waiter would ya please come take our order, we been waiting here fo da longest now. What would you like to order Sir? Hum let me see here from this menu, Miss Jennifer Main you go fust. Well Ok! James dear and let me sees here now, I believe I'll have the fried chicken, biscuits and gravy.

And now you sir . . . . Lets me see here . . . Let me have a buffalo steak about this big and this thick. Well, how would you like it cooked sir? With fire of course why . . . silly . . . Oh come old man ya think I'm stupid or something, I wants it cooked lightly on both sides and raw in da middle? Oh! I see sir, you want it cooked rare. What in tar nations ya talking bout man I didn't say I wants it cooked rare, I dun said, I wants it cooked brown on both sides and raw in the middle.

Well whatever you say sir and what size you showed me again sir? I dun measured with my hands . . . THIS BIG. Well sir I'm afraid we don't even have a plate in the house or this whole town to hold a stake that big Sir but I'll a sure ya our cook will do their best to accommodate you. And what would you both like ta drink, sir and madam? I'll have tea if you got it! And you sir what would you like ta drink? Ya got any liquor? No sir we don't have any strong spirits here.

Well tar nations man there ya goes again! I didn't ask ya if-an ya had any ghost or not, I dun asked ya, did yaw have any liquor, wine, or maybe some beer. Jennifer says, now James I'm surprised at you! Well sir we do have the best tasting apple and peach cider in town. Is any of it fermented? Why no sir. Well then dat blamed it, I guess I'll try some of that nasty tasting old tea too, I guess. That's the nastiest tasting old stuff a body can ever put in their mouth.

Would either of you like to have dessert? Yes we would. We both would like a piece of apple pie! Why apple Jennifer, you know good and well, I don't like no darn apples. Well now James I'm really very sorry because, I really didn't know. Well what would you really like sir? Have ya got any watermelon? Well sir I tell you what, I know we don't, but I'll personally run across the street and purchase one just for you and don't even bother to show me how big a piece you want because, I can already guest for myself, I'll just bring you the whole thing and let you have at it and eat until your heart's content. Will there be anything else madam? Quietly Jennifer says, no thank you I believe that will be all for now.

Why thank you Ma'am, your food will be ready in just about an hour and a half!

*Why . . . I . . . I . . . could have
stayed at home and cooked faster than
that! Now James don't be so rude to the
waiter! Well now Miss Jennifer Ma'am
even you got-ta admit that, that sho tis
a terrible long spell of a time to be
waiting for vittals. Now James dear ya
gotta consider that there are other folks
here at this here restaurant and not just
us, and ya got-ta consider how it does
take a spell to get stuff fixed before ya
cook it good and proper like. I recon you
might be right, but I still think that
sho tis a long wait and I sho am hungry.
Now James, dear, while we're waiting,
let's talk! What ya want to talk about?*

*Why you and me silly, you and me. Oh!
Yes Jennifer let's do talk about me and
you . . . what do ya wanna knows? Well
tell me where ya come from and how ya got
here? Well Jennifer, honey I dun come from
out West and my folks had a little dirt
farm. My Pa and me and my five brothers
and eight sisters raised cone (cone means
corn) tatters and carrots.*

*"What's carrots?" asked Jennifer.
Carrots ain't ya never dun gone and
seen no carrots befo? No I ain't says,
Jennifer. Carrots something like a sweet
tatter but only dem long and skinny like
a sweet tatter, but dem long and moe
yellower than a tatter. Dem grow in da
ground just like a tatter or peanut or a
rooterbaker or something. How do ya cook
carrots 'Clem' or I mean James, now I
dun eat rotterbakers and peanuts before,*

but I ain't never saw or heard of no such thing as carrots. You sho you ain't joshing me James, Corn? Joshing ya now why ya think that Miss Jennifer cause I ain't joshing ya!

Did yawl have any farm animals James? We sho did! What types and how many? We had a whole herd of hogs and cows! Ya how many? How many what? Hogs and cows your pa had? Oh! He had bout seven or eight hogs I guess that he raised ever year fo eating and lard making. Oh, that was a whole bunch and how many cows did ya Pa have? Well just let me see here now, the last time I twas home hem had bout five or four, but by now Old Bessie probably dun gone and had her calf by now, so they got bout ten or twelve or so I recon.

Oh, that's nice James. Any of your brothers and sisters married? Yep they all are! How many grand kids your folks got? A whole bunch! Yeah, but how many James, don't you know? Why no I don't rightly know. Well why don't you know James? Cause I can't count! What you mean you can't count James? Well, Miss Jennifer, ya see Ma'am I ain't never been ta no school and I can't read nor write. You can't read or write, what you talking about James. If you can't read or write, tell me man how' did you make your order a few minutes ago? Well, Miss Jennifer Ma'am ya see that little old smartelic waiter dun gone and asked me what I wanted, so I told him.

Lord, Lord James, what do ya friends call ya? Some call me Carney, and others call me Cornbread and most young kids call me Mr. Con. Well tell me man do you even like corn? Nope I'm afraid I hate the stuff myself. You do, why? Cause when I was a little scraper I ate so much of the stuff until now I'm plum burnt out on it.

How did ya come way out here in the first place from out West James? Well I was passing through here once on a drive and kind of liked it here and I just came back later and stayed. You came on a drive, what kind of a drive James? A cattle drive, back a spell, a few years back! Tell me then why a strong man like yourself ain't married yet?

Cause don't no woman wants the likes of me and any haw I ain't gonna let no woman peck on me. Whatever on earth do you mean by you don't want no woman peckin' on a big strong man like yourself. (He rolls his eyes and says) I mean, I, ain't letting no lady get hitched to me and trying to make me like a rooster and try to hen peck me that's what. Why you saying that James? I think you're kind of handsome and charming. (he blushed) You do's my Lord, why think ya Ma'am.

Waiter oh, waiter is our food ready yet? Oh! Yes sir I was just about ta bring it over to your table. Well ya sho better hurry up, cause I'm bout ta loose my appetite after talking to this here lovely young lady here and you sho ya ain't got no beer or have's ya dun gone an dun drunk it all up ya self.

The food is brought out to us. Um, this chicken sho is good but I can just imagine that the dumplings would have tasted just as good or even better . . . how's your steak? It tastes rather well but it sho is tough. It musta come from the oldest bull or cow in the herd and it sho needs some moe salt and the tatters round it ain't cooked ta my likings either, they ain't even dun yet, here taste some. Now James you go on and take that fork down from my mouth; folks are beginning to look and laugh at us.

One day Jennifer came downstairs for breakfast and she waited until Amanda and Rob were gone. She told me and Joe she was going for a ride in town and a friend was coming to get her, but for some strange reason she hugged me and Old Joe in the kitchen and she told Joeson to come to her and she hugged him and lightly kissed him and there were tears coming down her face. That evening she didn't come home.

Amanda and Rob both wondered where she was. Later that night they waited up for her but no Jennifer. Rob inquired in town and at her school for days, but no answer. However they did learn that a month back she had finished the school but never told anyone. A few weeks later I was cleaning her room and noticed a note I had over looked earlier. I had found the note tucked under Jennifer's pillow. I called for Joeson to come read it.

He read it first silently to himself and tears began to fall from his eyes. He told me to go give the note to Ms. Amanda cause he didn't want to see her face when she read it.

Amanda and Rob came in and dinner was being served. I said, Oh, yeah Master Henry sir, when I was cleaning this morning I found this here note tucked under Miss Jennifer's pillow. Oh, let me have it said Amanda! No let me read it first myself and then you have a look see. Rob opens the neatly folded note and silently reads it to himself and anyone could see that sadness had come upon his face.

He refolded the note back into its original shape and he slowly and quietly handed the note to Amanda and left the table and went to the door and sat down on the front steps with his face in both his hands and it sounded as if he was crying. Rob, Rob said Amanda, what's wrong honey, what's wrong Rob? She opens up the note and began to read out loud:

Dear Manda and Rob please don't think I don't love the both of you because I do and I think you both for what all you done, done for me and I'm forever grateful to you both. First I want to apologize to you both for leaving without ever saying goodbye and by the time your house folks find this note and gives it to you, I'll be long gone. Now I know you want to know why I left. I'm in trouble—not with the law though. After I done had this child maybe I might get married but I just couldn't face you and tell you face to face. I'll be ok, Love Jennifer.

Amanda began to cry and I tried to comfort her. When the other slaves learned she had run-a-way they were sad also. On the back of the note she wrote these words; *if this child lives and if she had others she would name them after the people she loved.*

Amanda said she was running away again. It seemed like Jennifer was always running to or from something.

14

Four Loose Marbles

I believe this had to be one of Kate's favorite stories to tell because it really hit close to home.

Now that Doc Waters had an official office helper and his business was blooming; money was coming into his office by the buckets full. The little office he once had become too small and his new office has big fancy waiting rooms. He once only went to the bank to make small loans to make ends meet but now he went daily to make large deposits. He had now become one of the bank's largest depositors. Within a period of only three years, plantation owners were swarming his office with their slaves and animals. Many of his patients were bed ridden, crippled and driven with liver kind of diseases and illnesses. Mental illness had no cures at this time. The mentally ill would be locked away in their closets and kept out of sight of other people.

Because of being unlearned and uneducated, many strange superstitions were practiced. The belief in witches, devils, demons, hexes, spell binding and evil spirits was the norm. All types of mental illnesses were believed to have been caused by demons entering the victim's mortal soul. If a child was born with poor eye sight his mother or father had dabbled with the devil before the child was born and had seen him up close or far away.

If a baby was born with a cleft lips, the mother had kissed the devil or a demon before the child was born. The superstitions caused much of the crippling and mental disorders. They were believed to be caused by the mother or father's past life and the good Lawd above was punishing them through their children. Trinkets and good luck charms were worn by many to ward off evil spirits.

The poor and the rich alike always would nail and hang a horse shoe over their front door in order to keep out ghosts and bad spirits. If Doc Waters wanted to keep in good favor with many of his clients he had to go along with many of their beliefs. Waters, for peace sakes, himself carried around a rabbit's foot and he would often times let his patients see him rubbing it before he would care for them.

Many mothers would purchase dogs teeth from Doc Waters. The dead dog tooth would ward off teething pains if tied around a young baby's necks. If a black cat crossed someone's path during the day, they had to burn seven pieces of their clothing before the sun went down. The toad frog was the devil's helper and its urine caused warts. Waters even had a horse shoe over his door, just in case.

Mrs. Waters had now become a high fashion lady. Her silk dresses were shipped all the way from up north and a few even from Paris. Miss Carlen Ann Jones and Miss Sarah Lee Hawkins were invited to one of her house parties and they both were jealous and wondering where she bought such fine new clothes from.

The Waters only had one small carriage and a big gray horse for a long time. Now they owned two carriages and several horses for riding. The town society folks began to take notice about the seven large rooms Doc had added to his once run down looking shack of a house. None of the town's folks could figure out how they could afford a whole house and office full of new furniture.

Anita Riddles over heard the gossiping and jealous ladies and just smiled at them and said my Lawd, my Lawd. They now even had two little outhouses, one in the front of their house and the other one out back. Both of their outhouses had moon cut glass put in and a curtain put over the glass so you can peep out while you were doing your business. Waters was considering buying a little land and raising some stock of his own for selling.

Waters had many clients at least an hour's ride by horse back from his office and he left Joeson handling things until he returned. One evening business was slow and Waters was considering closing early and going fishing. Just as he had headed to his front door, Mrs. Flowers' son came running into the front door and saying Doc, Doc come quick Ma done turned for the worst Mrs. Flowers was one of Doc Waters bed ridden patients. When Waters arrived at her house about an hour later he found out she had had a heart attack. She died three days later from the heart attack and old age. While Waters had left to go see about Mrs. Flowers a lady came into town to be seen by him.

The lady had a lovely carriage to bring her to the doctor's office. The driver waited outside while she entered to see the doctor. No one seemed to be around or in the office. She began to say out loud, Is anybody here; Is anybody here? Doc Waters where are you at dear? Joeson was out back but heard her. He came inside to the front office and said,

Why excuse me Miss, but Doc Waters is out on an errand just now and won't be back until probably night fall. Oh ain't you Joeson? Yes ma'am I am; but Doc Waters ain't here just now. Can I tell him anything for you ma'am?

Oh no, he ain't here; why my stomach is hurting all over and, and I need to see a doctor something terrible. Miss I can go fetch him for you if you wants me to cause I knows where's he went. Now Joeson I done heard from my girls you know more about doctoring than you playing like. What you talking about Miss? You know what I'm talking about Joeson; my girls don told me before. What girls you talking about Miss? My girls out at my ranch, you recollect any black girls named Sally Mae, Anna Bell, Pearl, Sue and Sunflower.

He admitted he kind of did recollect the names. The woman started talking about all the girls at her ranch and how she sends them to him to be 'checked out.'

Again he admits that was she's sayin was true but he couldn't figure out what she wanted from him because he couldn't doctor on no white women.

She tried to convince him that it would be okay if nobody knew like nobody knew he could read and write. She asked him what he thought would happen if folks knew. He admitted that they might hang him.

She told him to close the door and put the closed sign in the window. She threatened him that if he didn't she just might tell all the white folks that he could read and a few other things that he wasn't supposed to know how to do.

Joeson closed and locked the door and asked what he needed to check. She told him that she needed to be checked all over but before he got started she wanted to know if it was true what they say bout men with big feet and hands like his. Joeson asked her what she meant by that. But she said she was gonna see for herself. She told him not to close his eyes or turn his back just because she was taking loose her dress for him to check her. She told him to come closer to her and don't be scared. She asked him if he had ever seen a naked woman before. He told her yes but me ain't never seen no naked white woman. She said buck naked black girls and white women all look the same and the only difference is the color of the skin. She urged him to touch her and stop being so scared cause wasn't nobody there but her and him and the door was closed shut good. She showed him where to touch her cause that was where it hurt, at her stomach. Joeson told her he wasn't gonna to do it cause he was scared. She told him to give her his hand and don't be scared because ain't nobody gonna know cause she wasn't gonna say nothin to nobody. She gave her promise.

She told him to push real hard on her belly because it hurts so bad. He asked her what she been eating. She said cabbage, raw onions and a few glasses of beer. He told her that maybe that was the cause of her stomach hurting. He said she probably had gone and got the floats (Floats-gas). He offered to go fetch her some medicine they had made up for that ailment and it would help her to cut it loose.

She told him that she had something else ailing her and she needed him to come closer so she could hold him and rub on him a spell to repay him for taking care of her. She said, my Lawd, my Lawd, it is true what they say about big feet and big hands

The lady was the town's madam and outcast. Her name was Miss Sara Lee Hawkins. She usually received money from men, even on occasions from Doc Waters for the services she had given to him, if you know what I mean. On this occasion she gave Joeson three gold pieces for the services he had given her and all the way home she was smiling and saying, "It's true, it's really true; what they say about big feet and hands." I know curiosity killed the cat. The money wasn't for the medicine he gave her;

it was for something else she persuaded him to do to her; "If ya know what I mean!"

At the end of the fifth year, many of the poor white folk were beginning to show deep signs of jealousy at church. There had been rumors sent back to Annabel that there had been secret towns meetings held questioning whether or not they should burn the Waters' house and office to the ground. Hatred was beginning to show up its ugly head because Doc Waters had been asked by several of the town's folks if he would consider training one of their sons how to become a doctor. Waters always responded with yes Sir or Ma'am, and told them he would get back them and let them know, but he never did.

At one of the secret meetings, two old men, Clifford Baxter and Old Man Maxwell spit out their tobacco and said that Doc Waters had him a slave, of all things, helping him and working for him for nothin while the good town's people are making him rich.

Miss Hassey Breadcrums lashed out and said that she had asked him more than once if he would train her son Franklin how to doctor folk, but that he didn't never got back to her. Crabgrass stood up and said yeah that all of them can see good and well what that no account Waters had gone and done to him.

Miss Sara Lee Hawkins said to Mr. Crabgrass that all of them knew Doc Waters had to take off his left leg, but that they also knew that it had festered with what they call gang green. And she told him if he could learn how to cut wood and not his dat blamed foot half way off with his axe and then not let his foot fester way up his leg, Doc wouldn't have had to cut his leg off.

Miss Hawkins asked if she could say something even though she wasn't nothin but a lady. Sally Mae piped up and said they had all heard tell what kind of a lady she was! Somebody told Sally Mae to sit because they wasn't there to judge Miss Hawkins, they were trying to do something bout Doc Waters and that slave he got working for him for nothin. They kind of thought he had done gone and trained Joeson before he even considered training one of their sons. They told Miss Hawkins to go on and say what she had to say and that she better be quick about it.

Miss Hawkins reminded them that the good book says you should love your neighbor as yourself but that they sure wasn't showing no kind of concern in her opinion. Now the way she looked at it, Doc Waters had helped more folk than he done harm to. She asked for an agreement. She went on to say that Doc Waters had brung more children in the world than they could shack a stick at, even her.

They said they agreed but someone said she ought to try to use the good book for her own defense, especially after the things they been hearing that she been doing out at that old ranch. She said never mind bout her ranch cause she ain't dragging the men folk over there cause they all came on their own. She told them women that they ought to start giving their men folk more milk at home they would stop going to the cows out at her ranch. She said that as she recalled that one of the women and her four daughters had worked a night or

two themselves out at her ranch to make some
extra money. She was called a hussy and asked
who she was trying to tell on. A brawl almost
broke out but the meeting had to go on.

The real thing is if Waters done trained
that slave boy surely he better train one
of theirs. They should at least give Waters
another chance. They came up with a scheme
to test Walters by having a couple of the
women folk next week over to Waters office
and play like they were sick and during the
conversation ask him to train one of their
sons how to doctor folks to see what he would
do and in a few weeks they would see if they
needed to handle him

Through the grapevines Waters heard of the
plot to burn and tear down his office and
house. He hired two white helpers and most
of the contentment ceased. One of the boys
he hired was named Franklin Breadcrumbs and
the other ones name was Thomas. Franklin was
only a poor farm boy. He began work for Waters
for the easy money. His family was dirt poor.
Thomas' family was of a higher class category
than Franklin's. Thomas' folks owned many herds
of cattle and his Pa was a plantation owner.
His Ma had a sewing business. His parents had
servants working for them.

One of the town's folks came by the Henry
Plantation and purchased two new horses. They
were laughing and talking to Rob about the plan
to destroy Waters business and hang and kill
the slave he had working for him. Rob asked
them why and they told him the reason. The men
never knew that Joeson was Rob's slave and Doc
Waters and Rob were the best of friends.

Doc Waters had the same mission he had originally with Joeson; trying to train his new helpers. Neither of the two new helpers was really interested in doctoring folks. Everyday Waters and Joeson were constantly engaged in trying to operate a business while Thomas and Franklin were only making trouble. Joeson would try to help both of the boys learn their new trade of doctoring and making medicine but because of Joeson being a slave and not being paid, they paid little attention to whatever he had to say to any of them. They paid him no never mind. Daily if anything went wrong, the blame was always placed on Joeson. On numerous occasions Franklin and Thomas would get in the front of Joeson and make statements that they really didn't need Joeson around and they could get along just fine without him:

They questioned why Waters keep him on in the first place was past their understanding. The two trouble makers were green in the job of making medicines and when Waters was out doing his rounds they would sneakily ask Joeson for advice in how to handle different cases and causes. However now that Thomas and Franklin were on the job, Joeson now only took care of cleaning and sweeping floors and caring for the animals that the boys didn't want to care for. When plantation owners brought in a slave for care the only time Joeson cared for them was if they had any type of serious illness or sickness that the trouble makers were afraid of catching.

Despite the uneasiness in the office, Thomas had been saving up his money to attend the medical school in the big city just like Doc Water had done. One morning Joeson arrived at the office and learned that Waters had to leave town in a hurry, because his mother had taken ill.

Waters had to be gone for a whole week and a half. Franklin and Thomas were in charge while Waters was away. The day after Waters left started off with a big bang. Two armed robbers had held up the town's bank. The bandits got captured and shot in a shootout. A mob of men had brought both of the wounded robbers over to the doctor's office only to find out that Doc Waters had left to visit his sick mother and had been gone for a whole day.

The trouble makers took the men into the operating room and told the towns folk to stay outside while they performed their operations. Joeson, Franklin and Thomas, all were together in one room performing the operations. Joeson was on one table alone by himself and Franklin and Thomas were working on the other robber by themselves.

As Joeson was performing an operation and removing the bullets from his man's chest, stomach and leg, he was also trying to tell Franklin and Thomas how to save their wounded man but they refused to hear what he had to say. Joeson's man lived through the operation but Franklin's and Thomas's man died on the operating table. After the operations were finished someone had to go outside and tell the towns folks what had happened.

Franklin told Joeson to stay hidden in the back office while he went outside and told the towns people the news that one of the men had died on the operating table but they had saved the other one and if Doc Waters had been there they may have been able to save the other. The town's folks all praised both of the new young workers and said they both had done a good and fine job and one day they both would be fine young doctors.

The next day Doc Waters came back to his office and heard the news of what had happened from both Franklin and Thomas, but behind Joeson's back they claimed that the robber on Joeson's table had died. Doc Waters asked Franklin and Thomas did the town's folks know that Joeson had operated on a white man and that he had died.

Both boys told Waters that they had kept it secret and they had told the town's folks that they had performed the operations. Waters left the office in a sweat and a worried look on his face. He went for a big strong drink over at the saloon but before he left he asked the two boys did they know that if the town's folks had known that Joeson had killed a man, a white man of all things, both of them might get hung and the very least they might do to him was burn down his office and run him out of town.

At the saloon he was taking him a few shots of liquor while he listened to a few of the good old boys tell him what they saw happen. They assured Waters his helpers had did a fine job on operating on both of the bandits. They suggested that if he had been around maybe both of the crooks may have been saved.

They said if the two young helpers hadn't of been there no one would have been saved cause they all knew good and well that the little old stupid black floor sweeper slave didn't have sense enough to do nothin. He was only good to rub down a few mules or horses and maybe remove a few ticks or lice from one of his own kind. They both laughed and said they didn't see why Doc got that boy there for anyhow. They said he ought to be out in the fields picking cotton with his own kind and if he didn't have a job here in town with the good white folks he might be a good liberty stable boy cleaning out stalls for the good white folk's horses, mules and such. One of the men named Ed asked Doc to buy him a drink.

He then turned around and asked if it was true darkies really have tails that come out at night. Doc said to him that he knew all darkies don't have tails, only the blue eyed ones. Well tell us this then Doc, is coons like him hard to raise? Doc asked him what he meant. He said can you tell him to go fetch a stick like his old blood hound, Red Bone? Doc laughed and said ya, ya, ya he can fetch just like your hound.

Doc began talking with another drunk, and said he reckoned he was right bout that darn old darkie he had working for him, that he ain't worth nothin much (hiccup). He asked him where they had buried that robber at. The man said well as for as they knew, they hadn't buried him yet. Another one said the other one is still in the town jail and shortly after he done mended good and well the Sheriff said he gonna hang him. Waters left the saloon with a grin on his face like an old possum and a bottle of whiskey in his coat pocket.

Later on that afternoon Doc Waters came back into his office in a rage and he called all of his helpers into his back office and they all sat down and had a really long talk. Waters got them to repeat to him the story of the robbers and who it was that had operated on who?

The two trouble makers told the same lie all over again and they refused to let Joeson say anything. Doc Waters told them he had went and examined the live wounded robber in jail and he went and also examined the dead man before they had buried him that morning. He told them that the living man had a fair chance to live on his own not considering the operation he had got but he could have had a better operation.

Both of the trouble makers started to smile until Doc Waters said he had to tell them all something. If I knew who operated on that dead man I'd hang him myself. Franklin and Thomas asked Doc why he said that. Doc told them that man didn't die from his minor gunshot wounds; he died from the sorry operation he got. As usual Franklin and Thomas put the blame on Joeson. Waters just shook his head told them to just call it a day and let everyone go back home.

The following weeks for Joeson were pure hell and everything was going downhill for him. Doc Waters was on his back constantly yelling and swearing about getting rid of him. Everyday Joeson would ride back home with his head hung down and his tail tucked between his legs. Now the only thing the mere floor sweeper wanted to do was somehow leave Doe Waters operation and never come back. The problem was that he didn't know how.

Early one morning Joeson was in his back room wishing he was back on his Master's plantation doing anything but working for Doc Waters and having to put up with Franklin and Thomas' insults. A soft knock came from the outside of his window. His back was turned and he turned to see who or what it was. The knock came again and as he turned to see who was talking to him, he could see that it was a woman.

The knocker outside of the window said softly, *"Mr. Joeson, please sir please help me."* Joeson went to the side door and asked what was wrong and told her to come in. As the lady came inside she had a little child with her and Joeson plainly could see that she was a slave. She explained to Joeson that her Master's wife had allowed her to come see him. Her Masters' wife only knew that the slave woman's young daughter was ill and needed help.

Joeson saw the child that was with her and it appeared to be scared and in lots of pain for some reason. Joeson told the mother and child it was okay he would do all he could for the child. He asked the child what was wrong and she pointed to her head and stomach. Joeson told the child to calm down and he would try to ease her hurt.

The child had a bad tooth. Joeson talked softly to the little girl as he told her to open her mouth and close her eyes as he quickly pulled the bad tooth. She yelled and began to cry some but her mother told Mae Sue not to make no trouble for the man. Joeson only laughed and said that it was okay because old man Waters and his old white helpers were all gone.

The woman said, *Thank the Lawd."* She reached up and hugged Joeson around his neck and thanked him. As they were leaving, Joeson told her to make sure that the little girl didn't eat nothin on that side for a few days.

The woman asked Joeson if she could ask him something before they left. He told her, sure she could. She asked him if he would check something else for her.

The woman began to cry then the little child did too. The woman told the child that she ought not to say nothin because she just might be in the woman's way.

Joeson was confused about this saying and questioned the woman some more. She looked at Joeson sadly and said she done been bleeding a whole bunch lately. He said it was okay she was gonna stop in a little while cause he found out that most women folks do that. The child spoke up and said that her mother hadn't told him why she was doing that. He told the little girl that just because he was a man he still knew what he was talking about. He asked her how old she was and she said she didn't know but her mother would know. He then asked the mother. She said as far as she could recollect that the girls was about seven or eight years old. Joeson repeated what he had heard and said that the child was a bit young to be bleeding like that. She said, yes sir.

Noise began to come from the front room
and Joeson could hear Waters and the trouble
makers talking. Waters, Franklin and Thomas
entered the room and teased Joeson about
finally getting a patient. They asked what
plantation the woman was from. The mother said
they were from the Crowder plantation. Doc
wanted to know what they came to see his black
helper for. She explained that the child has
bad pains.

Franklin still didn't understand. Doc Waters
told Franklin and Thomas to go and tend to
the business out front while he tended to the
problem. After they left for the front, Doc
said to Joeson that he could see something
was wrong from the look in your eyes. Joeson
said that the child had a bad tooth and he had
yanked it for her. Doc told him that he had
done a good job and he could go over to the
Crowder Plantation and collect his nickel for
pulling one of his slave's teeth. The mother
begged him not to do that. Doc wanted to know
why he should do that and pressed her to tell
him what she was leaving out.

Franklin and Thomas came inside the room
and were about to interrupt but Waters asked
them where their manners were; to knock before
entering. He asked them what they wanted. They
apologized and said it could wait. Doc told
them not to come back later and to head down
to the town kitchen and order some dinner
for all of them and wait until he got there
before they started eating. He went back to
the girl and her mother about why he shouldn't
tell their Master that they had come to his
office.

They said that if he knew he might beat his wife because she was the one that let them come to see Joeson. He said okay and agreed to keep quiet and not say anything to Old man Crowder. He knew from the past that Crowder was certainly a grump. The little girl began to cry and beg her ma to please tell the white doctor for her. Doc wanted to know what the child was talking about. He asked the child where else was she was hurting still. The child pointed and said,*" Down here."*

Waters asked Joeson had he checked her down there and he said no. He asked why he hadn't checked. He said because her mother said she was in a woman's way. Doc asked him what he meant. He said he was talking about her hard bleeding. He asked how old she was and the mother again said she was seven or eight. The Doc was shocked to hear her age (just like Joeson was) because that wasn't right for being in a woman's way. He said he needed to check her out. Waters took the child and her ma to his front office and told Joeson to go close the door and put to closed for business sign out.

Joeson questioned him but he told Joeson to just do what he said. He said to close the door so that no white folks could come in while he was seeing about that child. After about half an hour Waters came out of his office with a disgusted look on his face. Joeson asked him what the matter was. Joeson could hear the sound of the child's mother crying in the front office. Waters looked at Joeson and said the child's mother is crying because her child had died in his office.

Joeson could hardly believe what he heard. He wanted to know how she could walk in there okay and now she was dead. Doc said that she had bled to death. Bled to death, Joeson said, more confused than ever because she shouldn't have bleed to death from a tooth yanking! Doc Waters said he knew and told Joeson to take a quilt and go wrap up the child and give her back to her ma. The mother took the dead child and carried her back to her plantation and they buried her.

After they had left Waters told Joeson not to worry because in their business they see a lot of people come and go, it's a way of life. Joeson went home that afternoon and told his folks, Old Joe and Kate, what had happened that day and he was sorry that he had pulled that child's tooth and she had bled to death.

Waters went home and had dinner with his wife Annabel. Annabel asked her husband what was wrong because all afternoon he looked like he had seen a ghost. He said he had and to tell the truth he wished it was only a ghost that he had seen. He told her how he had examined a little girl and she had died on his exam table. Annabel was shocked and asked what was wrong with her. Doc told her Joeson had pulled one of her teeth but she was hurting real bad so he took her in my office to see what else was bothering her and she was bleeding heavy and she died on my exam table.

She told him, it wasn't nothin that big because she had to be a slave if Joeson had pulled her tooth. He said yea but what he didn't tell Joeson was that she hadn't died from having a tooth yanked. Annabel asked what she died from. Waters said the little girl had been raped. Annabel was out done because rape was a crime.

Doc confirmed that the poor little child had been raped. Before he examined her she told him what her Master's grown sons had been doing to her for the past few weeks. The poor child just couldn't take it anymore. Annabel felt so bad and wanted to know how old the child was. He told her that she looked to be no more than eight or nine years old. He told Annabel that it just broke his heart and her ma couldn't do or say nothin to her Master cause he would have had her beaten or who knows what. Annabel said that maybe one day God was gonna help those poor things. She asked Doc if he was gonna tell the sheriff. Waters said what good would it do because he wasn't gonna do nothin about no slave girl being raped. Old man Crowder would laugh in the sheriff's face if he was even asked about it. She told him that no matter what he said, first thing in the morning she was going to the sheriff's office and report it.

Two days later Annabel went by her husband's office and told him what the sheriff had to say. She asked him if they could go somewhere alone to talk privately. He said sure just as soon as he finished with his patient. They stepped into a side room where they could be alone and talk privately. She told him her feelings were hurt. He asked her about what because he didn't remember saying anything lately to her. She assured him that he was not to blame but the sheriff was the one.

When she told him about that poor little slave girl that had been raped, he said he could care less about her or any other darkie getting raped and he wished she would stop wasting his time with such non-sense. When she asked him what was he going to do; he started to laugh and said nothin, what did she think he was going to do? She asked him if he was even going to arrest Old man Crowder's sons for what they did.

He began laughing even harder and spitting that old nasty tobacco and got some of it on her new dress. He told her that it was okay for a white man to do whatever he wanted with his slaves cause they were his property and can't nobody tell a slave owner what to do or what not to do with his own property. He told her that just for her knowing that if a darkie ever raped a white girl or woman he wouldn't arrest them either because he would skin them alive and then hang him later after he had cut off his private parts.

As autumn arrived and leaves began to fall from the colorful trees, many squirrels were at their busiest harvesting acorns and nuts. Joeson could see the wood ducks and the snow geese in flight headed further south for winter as he rode into town one dusty morning. The wind blew hard against his face as he stepped down from his horse and tied it to the rail. There seemed to be music coming from the inside of Doc Waters' office.

Joeson stepped into the office and saw that there were a few towns' folks in Waters' office. Thomas was being given a goodbye celebration. Thomas had decided to go to the big city school of doctoring to study just like Doc Waters and become a doctor on his own. Joeson was never offered anything to eat or drink but after the party was over and everyone had left Thomas did come over and shake Joeson's hand and wish him well.

The day before Thomas left he came by the office to say a final goodbye to Doc Waters, Franklin and Joeson. Thomas asked Waters did he remember any of the teachers names when he went to school. Waters said he had forgotten all of the teacher names that had taught him because it had been such a long time ago. Thomas only smiled and said he'd tell all the professors and teachers that Doc did good after attending their school. They all shook hands and Waters thanked him. He asked Thomas do him a favor and not to even mention his name when he got up there. Thomas said okay if that's what he wanted. Thomas rode off waving goodbye.

Waters had asked Thomas not to mention his name at the school not because he had become old and maybe forgotten. Waters' real reason was he had never been to that or any other big fancy school of doctoring. Waters had lived in the town where the school was located. He wanted to attend the school but his family was too poor to send him.

He had a friend that had a wealthy family that did attend. The friend on weekends would invite Waters to his house and privately teach him. After graduation his friend later returned back and became Dean of the school and still remained there, and Waters knew it. Waters had learned the trade of doctoring well. Most of his understanding came through trial and error.

The town he now practiced in never investigated his past but they all trusted, loved and respected him. Waters had one more skeleton in his closet in the town where the school was. Waters had a woman he had left for another woman and three little children. The woman was his wife and he had deserted and left. His ex-wife was the sister of his friend and still the Dean of the school.

Doc Waters went along with the town's folk and wished Thomas well, but he knew something was awfully fishy about Thomas going off to school so early. Doc Waters' office had been broken into and robbed a few times back but the thieves had never been caught. Money was the only thing stolen. The thieves always seemed to know just where the cash box was hidden.

After each of the robbery, both Thomas and Franklin would come in the next day with sneaky and unconcerned looks on their faces. A short while after the robberies each helper would come to work wearing new clothes and boots and have a pocket full of money.

Once, Doc Waters had to take Franklin home early because he had turned a little ill. Waters came inside of the little shack of a farm house and noticed some of the wooden carved animals on the mantle of Franklin's mother's fireplace.

After Franklin had laid down, both of his parents came outside to talk with Doc Waters. Both parents only laughed when they learned Franklin had eaten too many green apples. Waters complimented Franklin's mother on the pretty little wooden painted animals she had in her house.

He asked her where he could buy such pretty things. The parents said they didn't know where their son had got them from all they knew was he brought them home on several different occasions. They said that once he even had a pocket full of money that he claimed to have saved up and he shared it with his other brothers and sisters.

Now that Thomas is gone many of Joeson's problems had eased up some. Franklin knew that he couldn't make it without a side kick. Franklin tried to get Doc Waters to hire another helper. A twenty two year old named Larry Joebell was the new helper's name that Franklin brought in but Waters ran him off on the third day. He seemed to like the taste of the medicines that were made from corn whiskey.

Waters made mention of getting himself another slave and letting Franklin go and Franklin soon forgot to mention the idea of getting another sidekick. Events were about to take place in Joeson's life that are going to make a dramatic change forever. Almost an entire year has passed since Thomas had left for medical school.

All three of the medicine men were walking together in town and had almost completed their rounds and were headed back to their office when a large group of school kids came running up to Doc Waters and yelling for the Doc to come quick. They said that "Red" was gonna die, she's gonna die, come quick! Several of the smaller children grabbed Franklin by his hands and britches and dragged and shoved him.

The three men ran with the young kids down the main street, turned passed the bank, ran down Jones Street and finally down to the town's school playground. From a distance the three could see all of the towns' people that had arrived at the school playground to see what the commotion was all about but the three couldn't see what was going on.

Someone began to yell out that Doc was coming and everybody needed to get out of his way so he can help her. The large crowd opened up for Waters and his helpers to come into the center of the ring. There, lying on the ground was a little red headed girl who appeared to be gagging and choking to death on something she had swallowed.

The scene was like when the school bully had been backed downed and dared by a brave underdog but everyone still was cheering for the underdog to win. A huge circle would be made around them so everyone could watch. The town's emergency bell had just begun to ring and everyone was coming to see what was wrong. The saloon was closed down and the barmaids were all out looking. The bank doors were closed and the money lines had all dispersed and the account holders had ran to the playground and were watching the child on the ground choking to death.

Doc Waters broke through the huge circle and started asking what happened, what had gone wrong. One of the young kids answered and said, almost out of breath and heart beating real hard, "Doc, Doc she was playing marbles with us and when we wasn't watching, she went and put a handful in her mouth and now she done

choked on them." Franklin yelled and demanded
to see her to see if he could put his finger
down into her throat and maybe just push them
down. Franklin tried his idea but she only
choked worst. Doc Waters tried patting her
hard in her back but still she only gagged
worst. Finally the poor child's ma and pa
arrived after hearing the news.

They both were screaming and yelling, 'Oh
no, what we gonna do? Lord, Lord, what we
gonna do?" The town's preacher and church folks
were down on their knees praying out loud.
The little girl's eyes were falling back into
her head and she had begun to turn blue from
the lack of oxygen and her breath was slowly
leaving her.

Waters and Franklin were trying to do
everything they knew to do to revive the child
but they were failing miserably. It appeared
that all of their efforts were all to no avail.
Joeson yelled out despite the fear for his own
life but in sincere concern for the child's
life.

He begged Doc Waters to listen to him for a
moment. He told the Doc that he knew something
that might save her if he would listen to him.
Angrily, Franklin lashed out with fire and
brimstone telling Joeson that if he and the
Doctor can't save her what made him think he
could with his black stupid self.

Joeson cried out again because he could see
that the situation had become desperate and
life threatening. He said he knew for sure
what to do to save the girl if somebody would
only give him a chance because the same thing

had happened to him before. He pleaded for
somebody to please listen to him.

The little girl turned bluer until finally
her mother screamed out in desperation. She
damned them all to hell and asked why don't
they at least listen and maybe give the black
boy a chance because nobody else seemed to know
what they were doing. The child's pa boiled up
and spit out his rattle snake like venomous
poison and said ain't no black boy like that
gonna touch no child of mine and especially no
slave. He threatened his wife to wait until
they got home, for saying that anyhow. He spit
in the black man's face. Joeson wiped the
child's father's spit and tobacco from his
face and turned around and headed back to his
office in a hurried walk.

Joeson turned the corner from the crowd and
turned and said softly he only wanted to help
and a few tears began to find their way down
his dark cheeks. The little girl's life slowly
began to fade away. One could see lumps in her
neck as two of the marbles protruded under the
skin and two others were lodged in her wind
pipe.

She was strangling to death. Doc Waters
effortlessly tried to dislodge the marbles
by rubbing them down but it only seemed to
make matters worse and cut off her air supply
even more. Looking totally frustrated, Waters
fessed up and said there wasn't anything else
he knew to do.

He said that the poor child was just going
to die and he was sorry. All the folks were
told to stand back and let her parents come
round to see her before she died. A total

silence came upon the whole crowd as the sadden parents came crying to see the life being snuffed out of their child and it seemed as if nobody could do anything about it.

The child's mother screamed and cried out as her husband tried to calm her. Franklin sadly said they were sorry but just like they said, ain't nothin they knew to do but let her poor little girl die. The mother held her child and asked what about the slave boy.

The child's pa yelled out again that ain't no black slave gonna touch no daughter of his. He said that he would die and go to hell first. Her Ma wept and said that they had to be some of the damnist and stupidest people on God's green earth; if they can't save her at least they could give that black slave boy a chance because their daughter was dying.

The little kids run up to the child's pa and begged him not to let "Red" die just give her a chance to live. Finally he said okay someone go get him and let him at least try to save her. The crowd yelled out for the girl's pa to at least give Joeson a chance. The protest was quieted down when the ma yelled out and said she didn't care whether he was an animal, horse, cow, mule or dog or cat doctor. It really don't make a hill of beans, all that mattered to her was if he could save her little Mary Lou.

Many of the little children had run down the street and were trying to find which direction Joeson had left in. They finally found him half way to Doc Waters' office. The little kids crowded Joeson and got him by the hand and led him back to the scene at the playground. When he arrived, the Ma yells *"Thank ya Lord.",* *"Thank ya for your mercy."* She turned to Joeson and told him to go on and give it a chance.

The girl's Pa raised up and tried to attack Joeson, but a few of the men standing by stopped him and held him. He still managed to say, *"now boy you better hear me well, I want you ta know straight up front if you touch my daughter and she dies we gonna hang ya, okay?"*

Waters told Joeson that he didn't have to even try if he didn't want because if she dies they gonna hang him. He urged him to think twice before he tried. Even Franklin told Joeson that it was okay if he didn't try. Joeson softly said, maybe it's time for him to die cause ain't nothin worth living for in this world anyhow and he was at least gonna try.

The scared black slave doctor knew his life weighed in the balance, but he was sure he knew what he was going to do. He walked over to the choking half dead little girl and someone yelled out get the ropes ready boys cause they was gonna have a coon hanging that night.

Joeson kneeled down next to the child and put his left hand under her neck and his huge right hand under her thighs and picked her up and he looked toward heaven as if he was going to pray but he dropped her head and let it hang down as he held her heels with his huge right hand. She still cried and choked as he began to swat her back.

Her father broke loose from the men that were trying to hold him and he ran up and was about to grab Joeson as he saw two of the marbles falling from his daughter's mouth. He

stopped and was in awe as he saw Joeson give
his daughter a few more swats and the last two
marbles fall from her windpipe and mouth. A
total of four marbles had been swallowed but
now they were loosed. Four loosed marbles.

The crowd began to applaud as the little
girl was starting to breath normally and ran
into her mother's arms. Franklin began to yell
out *"We did it, we did it, didn't we Doc
Waters?"* Doc Waters spoke up and said that had
not done it cause Joeson did it. He confirmed
that with Joeson by calling him *Doc Joeson*. He
told Joeson that he had made him mighty proud
and asked Joeson for his hand so he could
shake it.

The child's pa went up to Joeson, still
pretending to be a diehard, never thanking him
but he did take off his hat and looked Joeson
straight in the face as he pulled out his
handkerchief and reached up and began to wipe
off the tobacco he had spitted in his face.
He walked away with his head hung down. There
were many bystanders watching as he wiped the
poor black man's face and they were softly
saying that the child's pa ought to at least
tell that poor colored man thanks or even say
he was sorry or something.

Many of the church folks found the child's
Pa's behavior to be totally disgraceful; other
on-lookers only looked and laughed and said
don't no black, colored slave need no thanks
or deserve no apologies.

The little child's mother told Joeson that
she sure thanked him and said he sure knew his
doctoring and asked his name. She said she
didn't want to call him no boy because he sure

did prove himself to them. She wanted to tell
Master what a fine job he had done there that
day. She told him that the next day she was
going to bring over a basket of fried chicken
to Doc Waters' office and he could eat all he
wanted. She went on to say that in a few more
weeks their crops would be ripe and she was
gonna bring him over a couple of watermelons.

Dirty, sneaky old Franklin spoke up and said
his name was Joeson. Doc Waters told Franklin
they needed to give credit to whom credit was
due. Waters spoke up and said his name is *Doc,
Doc Joeson* is what I always call him. He let
it be known that Joeson was the best helper he
has and ever had.

An old lady came up to Joeson and said "*ya
know what son, I never thought I would put my
arms around a slave and especially in public*"
as she hugged Joeson and laughed. She said
"*Son ain't no one here more partial to ya than
me cause that little child ya just saved is my
only grandchild.*"

She wanted to know how he knew how to do
what he just did. She wondered if Doc Waters
taught it to him. He said no and explained
that when he was a young buck himself, he was
eating apples and the seeds got hung in his
neck and his Pa saw that he was choking and he
patted me in the back but it didn't help none,
so finally he turned me upside down and hit me
in the back and the seeds shook loose. The old
lady said she wondered why in the tar nations
didn't any of them think of that.

The child's pa now had walked through the
crowd and fetched his horse. He brought up his
horse with everyone looking and went up to

Joeson, excused himself and said he thought he owed him something for saving his daughter. He told him that the horse's name was Power. He said that Power was the only thing he had worth giving to anybody. He went on talking calling Joeson mister and asking him if he would please take Power, so he could say their debt had been settled. Joeson told him that he didn't owe him nothin. The girl's pa insisted that he did and said for Joeson to go on and take the horse. Joeson took the horse and everyone yelled out.

The three medicine men went back to the office. Waters and Franklin were reminding Joeson of what a fine job he had done. Franklin said he would be glad when the lady brought over the food. Joeson said he would be glad when she brought over the chicken but not the watermelon. Doc Waters asked him why he said that. Joeson said because he loved fried chicken but he wouldn't give a darn for no watermelon.

Franklin said he always thought all black people liked watermelon. Joeson left the room and went back to his own back office and said to himself that he didn't see or know why all white folks think black folks like watermelons.

The next day Franklin and Waters got into a fist fight and ended up with black eyes, busted lips, ribs, and half of their clothing half torn off. In the saloon a few of the towns drunks poked fun at them and said a black slave knew more about doctoring than they did.

The following morning Joeson rode into work and Doc Waters was out tending to his house patients and Franklin met Joeson at the door and told him Doc Waters was out doing his rounds but he had left him a message. The message was that he didn't need him anymore and he could go back to his plantation and began picking cotton again and never bring his ugly face back again.

Joeson asked him why Doc Waters would say such a thing because he always thought Doc Waters was rather fond of him. Franklin grunted out that since he went and showed them up with the white folks at the playground, they didn't need him anymore. Franklin said he told Doc they ought to first tar and feather him. He said that Doc said no that they would just get rid of his sorry no count black behind and he agreed.

Joeson turned and headed for the door with a sad and confused look on his face but he was smiling before he arrived home because he now knew that he was finally free.

15

Doc Joeson

Now that you know how a young negro slave came to be known as Doc Joeson, let me tell you how it really, really got started.

Rob was touched when Joeson told him he wished that he could learn how to doctor on folks like Doc Waters. Rob told him that when they get up to the house that he might just ask Doc Waters would he try to train Joeson how to doctor on the slave folks. He went on to say that maybe he could pay him or cut a deal with him. Of course, Rob was also thinking about how much money he could save every year and at the rate that the plantation was growing, it wouldn't take long before he would go broke paying the doctor bills every year, even if it was just once a year.

Dinner had been set for the fine medicine man. Amanda had her best society table cloth and finest china from upstate New York all set for a late supper eating. Flowers had

been freshly picked from Amanda's prize rose
garden and set in the center of the table. Her
great grandmother's punch bowl was filled to
the brim with freshly squeezed juices. Mrs.
Waters complimented her on the lovely candle
stick holders setting at each end of the
table. The fire in the fireplace was burning a
bright blue as the two men entered the eating
room. Mrs. Waters came for the first time with
her husband and spent the entire day with
Amanda. Mrs. Waters was totally spellbound and
speechless at the closets of fine clothes and
store bought furniture.

It was the first time that Waters' had come
inside of the Henry plantation house. Old Joe
and me began to bring out the trays and set
the table. The last thing the servants always
were taught to bring out were the meats. Grace
was said by Amanda; Rob didn't care that much
for church going and such. They all began to
pass around the trays of vittals and fix up
their plates. Amanda politely told us to bring
on the meat. Master Rob softly asked what kind
of meat was it. Mrs. Waters told him to just
wait and see. The covered dish of meat was
placed next to the punch bowl that was setting
near the center of the table. Doc Waters said
that he would go first.

After the meal was over, the guests were
escorted to the parlor and Rob and Doc Waters
both sat down in the old patchwork quilted
rocking easy chairs. They were handmade and
rubbed. Rob told Mrs. Waters that he had to
hand it to her and his wife for preparing a
good tasting meal and wanted to know which one
of the lovely ladies made that apple dumpling

pie. Amanda said it was her and why did he want to know. He said that he had never known before that she could cook so good. She teased him back by telling him that now he knew it.

Me and Old Joe brought in a tea pot and glasses for the two women and coffee cups for the men. Mrs. Waters asked Amanda where on earth they got all of those little things on their mantle. Doc Waters spoke up and said that he had to admit that the Henry's had about the prettiest plantation house and furniture he had ever seen. Mr. Rob thanked him and went on to say that his lovely wife Amanda was responsible for all the furnishings. Annabell asked if Amanda had bought all the lovely stuff. Amanda said she hadn't bought all those things but that one of their slaves had made it. Doc and Mrs. Waters found it hard to believe that one of the slaves had made all those things. Rob reassured him that indeed one of their slaves had made the things.

They told them that when Old Joe first showed them how he could make stuff out of wood they let him train the rest of his slave men and they all worked together at night and made everything they needed and wanted. Doc Waters said he believed him but it was just so hard to believe that mere slaves could make such pretty stuff.

The Doc wanted to know how in the world did Joe ever learned how to make such lovely furniture. He wanted to know if the salves had made the dining room table and chairs or did he buy them. Master Rob told him yes and that everything they saw in the house was made by the slaves. They invited the Waters to follow

153

them down to one of the wood sheds so they
could see for themselves that he wasn't lying.
Off they went. They saw that one of the slaves
was working on a hat stand and a pretty little
lamp table.

After the Waters returned they were both
amazed at what their eyes had seen; slaves
making store bought furniture. They had toured
the slave cabins and saw the fine stuff they
had made for themselves. Mrs. Waters said it
was truly amazing. She said how she would love
to have some of that stuff she had seen out in
the slave's cabins.

She said she never dreamed that she would
be envious of a slave's cabin, the handcrafted
chairs, beds and tables and such. She begged
Master Rob and Ms. Amanda to let the slaves
make some of that fine stuff for her and that
she would gladly pay for it. Master and Mrs
said that they would. Amanda told her that
before she left she would loan her a wagon to
take a few pieces over to her house.

Annabel asked if she could get a table like
Amanda had in the kitchen and the big fancy
bed she had up yonder in her bedroom or an
outhouse with a moon cut in the door like she
saw out back. Amanda said all she had to do
was ask them and they would see to it getting
made.

Rob told the Doc that when the pieces got
finished he would bring them over himself. Doc
Waters got a big smile on his face and said
that it would be mighty fine. Doc said that
since they had been so kind to them that he
couldn't find it in his heart to take any money
from them this time for the yearly checkup

for the slaves. The deal was sealed with a handshake. Then Master Rob told Doc Waters that he couldn't rightly let him to that because it wouldn't set right in his stomach and craw. He said it would be like accepting charity and he wasn't about to do that. Doc Waters pleaded with him to reconsider because it seemed like he was taking advantage of their fine southern hospitality. Rob told Doc Waters that he was going to pay him for checking his slaves but the furniture was to thank his wife Annabel for the fine meal that she cooked up.

They all sat and talked in the parlor into the wee hours of the night until they finally decided to head for their separate bedrooms. After the rooster had crowed the next morning and the last bit of sausage gravy had been sopped up and the coffee and tea pots had been drained; they all headed back to checking the other slaves.

Preparations were being made for the noon meal. Annabell was busy with Amanda deciding which pieces of furniture to load onto the wagon. Hours had passed into the morning and both of the ladies had become tired. Annabell asked Amanda if she would mind if one of the servants would fetch a bucket of cold well water and a dipper and glasses. As they continued looking and working in the barn; Joeson was there helping to load.

Joeson came up to Mrs. Waters and excused himself and asked if he could ask Annabell something. She looked at Amanda a bit puzzled as he questioned her, but she politely turned back to him and asked if he was addressing her. He said he was. She looked at Amanda

and told Amanda she didn't rightly know what
to say to this that there boy. Amanda said
it was alright because that boy was her son.
Annabell smiled and asked Amanda why she said
that slave boy was her son. Amanda simply said
that in a way he really was her son. Annabell
refused to accept that explanation.

Amanda whispered that maybe she would tell
her about it later in private when they were
all alone. Annabell turned to Joeson and looked
strangely into his big horse gray eyes and
finally she noticed that he also had slightly
curly straight crow black hair, even though it
was cut almost to the scalp, as if someone was
trying to cover up or hide something. She said
this child sure did favor somebody.

Mrs. Waters choked a bit and asked Joeson
nervously what he would like to know. Joeson
asked her what her husband said last night.
Annabell asked what in the world that there
black slave boy was going on about. Amanda
told Joeson to make himself more plain so that
she and Mrs. Waters could answer his question
more proper like.

He told them that yesterday afternoon he
told Master Rob that he wanted to learn how
to doctor using look learning instead of book
learning so he could doctor on people like
Doc Waters does. Look learning, what's look
learning, both women said at the same time.
Before he could answer, Mrs. Waters interrupted
him and told him to jump down from the wagon
he was loading so she could get a better look
at him cause he had her attention. She said to
Amanda to go hurry up and close the barn while

they have a little fireside chat with this young bright minded boy.

She asked him his name and Amanda spoke up for him. His name is Joeson; he was named after his Pa. She said that she was there when the child was born and she loved and cared for him when she first set eyes on him. She said she had always claimed him and when he was nothin but a baby when her husband would be gone out on cattle drives she took him from his mas arms at night and let him sleep with her.

She asked Joeson why in the Lord's name didn't he come tell her first before he went and told that darn old stubborn husband of hers. She said he should know that he could trust her and she wouldn't let nothin' bad happen to him.

Mrs. Waters said being a midwife is one thing but doctoring is another and even if she could persuade her old bull headed man into training him, ain't no white folks ever gonna let him doctor on them.

He said he understood but he could sure a lot of slave folk would come to him when they got sick.

Before Joeson could finish talking the servant had returned with the bucket of water, dipper and glasses and he handed them over to the ladies and asked was there anything else he could go fetch for them. They told him no and that he had done a fine job. They asked him to just step out for a minute or until they called him back.

Amanda told Joeson to continue on with how he wanted to help people. He promised to keep up on his chores and all. They told Joeson to

step outside with the other and wait until they
called them both back in just a short spell
while the women folk put our heads together
and fix this thing up for him. After he had
stepped out, Mrs. Waters said to Joeson to
close the door because they didn't want them
to be listening.

Amanda asked Mrs. Waters what her thought.
She said to Amanda to tell the truth she be
scared to death for Joeson but he certainly
seemed have good intentions. She wasn't sure
how the other white folks in town might take it
because a couple of some white kid's parents
wanted her husband to train their sons but it
always ended up going sour. She was afraid
that if a little black boy, and a mere slave
of all things, was given the same chance and
he really did succeed that her and her husband
might get burned out or run out of town.

Amanda said if Joeson was to get trained by
Doc Waters that there was no way that he was
gonna be doctoring on any white folks anyhow.
She asked her what she thought about Joeson
just work in her husband's office cleaning up
and watching what the Doc was doing while they
was there. Annabell agreed that that sounded
like a good idea.

It sure would be a blessing to our slaves
out here and many other plantations who became
ill to not have to wait for a whole year to be
cared for. Amanda said to Annabell that if her
husband was to train Joeson that she would make
sure that every year she would get new store
bought looking beds, tables, set teas and such
and anything else she wanted for her house for
the next three years. Annabell asked her did

she really mean all of the new furniture and
such that she wanted. Amanda assured her that
she meant it. Annabell said it was a deal and
to shake on it.

Rob and Doc Waters came inside the barn
instantly after they had finished shaking.
Waters asked why the wagon loaders were outside
resting. Amanda said she had told them to take
a break. The boys came back inside and finished
loading the wagon.

One evening Joeson and his folks were all
finished with the day's work and were resting
in their four room cabin. They all were
discussing what had happened that day. Joeson
had told what all he had loaded up for the
Waters' family.

We knew nothin of Joeson's hope of ever
becoming a doctor and he was very dismayed
about telling us. His tossing and turning
in bed that night made his parents sense
something was wrong. We went to his bed side
and questioned him. We could see the look in
his eye that day when he came back with Mrs.
Henry and Mrs. Waters from loading that wagon.
We told him that he could always tell us what
he had on his mind because we would at least
listen.

He got up from his patched sown quilt and
began to cry. We tried to claim him down so
we could find out what had gotten his heart
so torn and broken. He began to tell me that
he spoke with Ms. Amanda about how he wanted
to become a doctor, just like Doc Waters and
doctor on folks.

I told him that I understood why because
every slave child dreams to be free and to

become a big somebody like white folks. His
pa nodded in agreement. I began to hold him
and comfort him with some of my own tears. As
he held on to both of us, he said he wasn't
asking to be free because he didn't even know
what being free meant anyhow; all he wanted to
do was just to help folks. We asked him what
Ms. Amanda said after he questioned her.

He said she told him she was gonna take care
of it for him but that later she told him to
step outside of the barn door while her and
Mrs. Waters was talking but when he came back
in she didn't say any more about it. His pa
said that maybe he should not have said nothin
because he just didn't quite understand that
many of their people and folks had been beaten,
lynched and killed just for saying some of the
same stuff.

He went on to tell him that as far as they
knew Ms. Amanda seemed to be a mighty fine
lady but it was hard to tell for sure. He said
that most white folks couldn't be trusted no
further than you can see them. Another thing
was that white folks were funny; they seems to
be for you one day and the next thing you know
they would turned on you so he just needed be
careful what he said and did could they could
turn on him before he could blink his eye.

I told him that if he knew what we knew he
might just be better off to keep his mouth
closed shut. Joeson said that he believed Ms.
Amanda to be a truthful woman. I told him that
the good Lawd had some good white folks too
but it just wasn't many of them because most
of them were big liars.

Joeson challenged his Pa to tell him when he last seen a white person tell a lie. His pa told him that it was the day before when Master Henry came home and Ms. Amanda asked him if he had been out in the fields all day and he said yes. Joeson wanted to know how that was a lie. His pa said that when Master Henry came home that afternoon he smelled like cinnamon and his mouth smelt like that old moonshine liquor he loved to drink. Joeson still didn't get it and said to his pa that maybe he got drunk on some liquor out there in the fields.

His pa said if that was true, where the cinnamon smell had come from. Joeson confessed that he didn't rightly know but where did he think Master Henry got that smell from. Old Joe asked me the name of the woman that Ms. Amanda was always telling Master to stay away from.

I said Miss Sara Lee Hawkins. Joeson asked his pa what she had to do with Master Henry coming home early and smelling like cinnamon. His pa just told him that when he was older he would understand. Joeson still wanted to know how Master Henry was telling Ms. Amanda a lie.

He said he had seen Master Henry coming home early that morning and he was drunk and he asked him to fix him some bath water and he changed clothes and went out and got a little dirty and came back before Ms. Amanda came home and caught him. Now it clicked in how Master Henry had told a lie.

Joeson asked me if I believed his Pa was telling the truth about Master Henry or was he just joshing him. I confirmed that his a

pa wasn't joshing him. Now Joeson wanted to
know why his pa hadn't told Ms. Amanda the
truth when Master Henry told that big lie. I
simply said that there were some things that
are just better off not being told because the
truth could cause someone to get hurt or maybe
even killed in this case or they could end up
getting sold.

Joeson wanted to know how a lie could cause
somebody to get killed. I told him that I once
knew a slave Master that did the horse with
one of his slave girls. Joeson interrupted and
asked what I was talking about when I said,
doing the horse.

His pa asked him if he had ever seen the
dogs, cows, horses and other critters out in
the fields carrying on. He said he guessed
he kind of did now that he mentioned it. He
laughed and said that the Master had gone and
got the slave girl knocked up and he got a
man out of the fields to marry her and the
Master's wife believed the child she had was
by her slave husband.

Joeson said he could kind of see why the
Master did that because his wife might get
real mad and try to hurt him. Joeson asked who
I knew that had gone and done something as bad
as that. I told him that I would rather not
say but that if he knew, he'd be surprised.

I went on to tell him that we were trying
to say that Ms. Amanda seemed to be a mighty
fine lady but that we didn't know Mrs. Waters
so we couldn't rightly say. I told him to go
on to sleep and we was gonna pray for him to
the good Lawd above and that if the Lawd say
so that he was sure gonna get his wish.

Joeson said he wanted to tell them something before he went to sleep. He said just in case they didn't know before, some of their fellow black slave folks told some of the biggest lies and they sure can't be trusted either just like some of white folks. We said we knew and told him to go to sleep.

On the fourth day Waters and his wife left with their buggy and the loaned wagon loaded with furniture. A few weeks later, one night Joeson's folks were at his bedside and telling him not to fret so much because it just might not have been meant for him.

Joeson said sadly that maybe he just had his hopes up too high cause ain't no white folks gonna let a slave become no doctor no how. He began to doubt whether he would be good at it. His parents told him to just trust in the Lawd and if the Lawd wanted him to doctor on folks, he would make a way somehow.

I told my son that I had put off telling him something else and asked him to get up for a moment to come and sit down in the kitchen so we could eat a biscuit together.

I told him again that I had something to ask him. I asked what he would say or do if I told him that yesterday Ms. Amanda told me to keep it a secret from him that in a few days Doc Waters was gonna come and get him and take him to his house and let him start house keeping his office in town and he was gonna train him how to doctor on folks. Joeson was in shock and asked me if I was really telling him the truth. She assured him that it was the truth.

He could hardly believe what he was hearing. He thought I was just trying to make him feel

better. Me and his pa assured him that we
weren't trying to make him feel better; we
were telling him the truth. He told us he was
feeling better but he didn't believe them but
he was going to sleep so the both of us could
get some sleep too.

He heard his Pa say to me that he didn't
think the time was right to tell Joeson what I
had been aiming to tell him. Joeson asked us
what his pa was talking about. We told him to
go on and lay back down and I had something
else I wanted to tell him. He asked me why I
had water in my eyes.

I said it was because of what she wanted
to tell him. I asked him if he could remember
when we were talking awhile back and I told him
about the Master that did the horse with his
slave gal. Joeson said he sort of remembered
but wanted to know why I was asking.

I was crying now and Joeson was really
concerned. I said I was crying because maybe
is pa was right, this wasn't the right time
for me to tell him.

The next few days Master Henry and his wife
were still talking about Doc Waters and his
wife. Joeson was caring less and less for the
conversations. We were unaware that he had
planned to steal a horse and try to run away
to freedom. He had taken most of his clothes
and had hid them in the born in the piles of
hay. He knew the penalty for runaway slaves
was death but he would rather die than to
lose his dream of becoming a doctor. Days had
passed since he had, had the bedside talk with
his ma and pa but nothin had happened. Finally
the time had come that he would make his run.

He had saddled a horse and was tying his clothes in a bundle over the back of his horse when the scare of his life came. He heard a voice outside of the barn calling to him. The voice asked him if he was ready to go. The voice came inside the barn saying someone had seen him come that way. The voice was that of Doc Waters. He told him he could see that he was getting saddled up but he had his buggy outside because they was gonna take his buggy so he should go on and unsaddle that horse.

Doc Waters and Joeson soon arrived at his office. Waters hurriedly put Joeson to work cleaning his office. Patients came in and out and Joeson paid close attention to how the doctor treated each problem. Many of the patients had minor scrapes and bruise. On certain occasions gunshot wounds and stabbings would come in and that's when he learned what real doctoring was all about. He also learned that doctors were not God because they can't save everybody. Some of the patients would die despite what all was done.

Weeks of observing had passed and finally one afternoon Doc Waters told Joeson it was time for him to put down the broom and mop and he would begin teaching him how to make medicine. Joeson didn't understand what he meant about making medicine. Doc told him that finally nobody was around but the two of them and now he could show him what to do to help people.

He locked the door and put the closed for the day sign in the window. He told Joeson that they were going into his back room where can't nobody see. He told him first you got the take some of the liquid in the little brown jug and pour a certain amount into some smaller bottles. Joeson asked Doc Waters what was in the brown jug. Doc told him that the brown jug didn't have anything in it but good corn.

Joeson asked Doc what kind of corn is it that pours like water. Doc Waters said that he had forgotten that Joeson didn't know anything about corn liquor. He told him that in another bottle he had some wild bee honey. He went on to explain that when you mix corn whiskey and honey together you get cough medicine and it was good for croup too. He said for the ear ache, take some of the corn and mix it with olive oil.

He asked Doc Waters why he didn't know how to make corn liquor. He said he sure wish he could. Joeson asked him why he would want to know how to make corn liquor. He said if he knew how to make it himself it would save him a whole lot of money. Doc asked Joeson if he knew how to make corn liquor. Joeson told him, no sir but he had helped Master Henry a whole bunch of times out in the woods to make some.

Joeson caught himself because Master Henry told him not to ever tell. He apologized to Doc Waters and told him that he couldn't say any more. Doc Waters promised not to tell on him but said he would sure appreciate it if the next he helped would he please try to find out everything and come back and tell him. He told him that everything that he made needed to have some of corn liquor in it. He said folks like the taste and most women folks kept a bad cough so they could come back for more.

Joeson asked Doc what he sold that man today for the aches and pains he had in his knees and stuff. He told him it was a paste made out of goose grease, lard and liquor. Joeson asked Doc what was the stuff he gave to Miss Nancy for her tooth ache.

Doc made him promise not to laugh because it wasn't anything but black berry juice and corn liquor. Doc Waters said he thought Joeson would be good at making medicine. Joeson noticed that ever time Doc would sew up somebody that he would always pour something on their cuts and they would start yelling so he wanted to know what kind of stuff he was putting on them. Once again it was corn liquor with red berry juice to give it some color. Doc explained that corn liquor and whiskeys killed a lot of germs and eased pain and if it didn't ease the pain somebody only needed just take a little swig and it sure could make a body feel good and warm inside.

Joeson asked Doc if folks really drank that stuff. Doc said they sure do and went to get his shot glass so he could pour Joeson a little glass so he could see for himself. After taking a big mouth full and drinking it similar to water, Joeson grasped for his breath and said that the stuff was hot but it sure did make you feel kind of good inside.

Now the hiccups began. In between hiccups, Joeson told Doc he had one more question. He wanted to know what the white milk looking stuff was that Doc had poured in a man's eyes the day before. Doc was puzzled about what white looking stuff he was talking about. It came to him, he had removed a stick from his eye and he had poured the white stuff in his eyes before and after. He explained to Joeson that milk was the best thing to put in an eye to clean it out with and helped it to heal fast. Joeson told Doc Waters that he was gonna be sick. Doc was messing with him a bit and asked him what was wrong. Continuing to struggle with the hiccups, he said the liquor had made him faint and sleepy.

Doc told him he better not get sick from that little old shot of liquor and gave him another drink saying it would make him feel better. Joeson took the other drink and yelled to Doc that he was gonna be sick. Doc told him to hurry up and run outside. Joeson puked and gagged all over the floor and some splashed on the Docs clothes and glasses. Doc Waters wanted to get angry but began to laugh and said he sure didn't have to worry about Joeson drinking up his medicines when he wasn't looking.

Joeson settled down a bit and told Doc Waters he was sorry and was gonna mop and clean it up. Doc accepted his apology, but said under his breath said, never give boys men's toys. Joeson told Doc he needed to ask him another question before he had to go home for the day. Doc Waters said he thought they were through with questions for the day but to go ahead ask the question. Joeson asked him where he bought his liquor. Doc told him that he bought all his liquor from bootleggers and not to ask what a bootlegger was. Now Doc asked Joeson to let him know in advance the next time he felt sick at the stomach because he could give him something to help settle his stomach. Joeson said that he would try to remember next time

but what would Doc give him, he hoped it would
not be more of that stuff because he didn't
want no more of that liquor stuff. Doc said of
course not, he said he would beat up four raw
eggs with a spoon of red pepper. Joeson hurled
hard, puked, gagged and threw up again. Doc
asked if it was something like he said.

That afternoon Doc Waters had to help Joeson
to the door at the Henry plantation house. Rob
asked Doc Waters what was wrong with Joeson.
He told him Joeson had gotten sick at the
stomach. Rob told Joeson to go walk down to
his cabin and lie down. Rob walked Doc Waters
back to his buggy and just before he took off
he asked him was there anything he could do to
help settle Joeson's stomach.

Waters told him sure, just give him six raw
eggs beaten up and a teaspoon of red pepper. Doc
Waters was sniggering as he drove off because
he could hear Rob in the distant background,
gagging and puking. That night after a great
big super, Amanda and Rob were lying in bed
and he just happened to mention to her about
Joeson getting sick at the stomach at the
doctor's office. She asked the fatal question
of what Doc Waters said to give him to help
settle Joeson's stomach. Rob told Amanda she
didn't really want to know. Amanda insisted
on Rob telling her the cure. He warned her
that he told her she didn't want to know. She
raised up in bed to hear and Rob said Doc told
him that for the next three days everyday they
should take a whole peek basket of raw eggs
and beaten them up and add a cup of red pepper
and have him drink it and it would settle his
stomach.

She jumped up from bed holding her stomach and mouth raised the window and stuck out her head and the rest was history. Rob had his head tucked under the pillows laughing and saying he tried to warn her but she just had to know.

The next few weeks after Joeson had finished with cleaning the office Doc Waters would teach him how to make all sorts of remedies and cures for the most known illnesses and sicknesses. He gave Joeson many of his doctoring books he got from the school of doctors he had went to in the big city. Joeson secretly knew how to read but pretended not to. The pictures in the books would often time say a thousand words. When he could see the picture of a person's insides, the doctor's teachings were made clearer. At the end of every day, Joeson usually would have a few questions to ask.

One afternoon before leaving for the day he asked a rather comical question and got an answer he really didn't understand. He wanted to know what was the greasy brown funny smelling stuff he had made up and given to Mr. Talltree. Doc Waters asked him if he meant the axial grease, liquor and castor oil. Joeson nodded that indeed that was what he was talking about. Doc said it was for the piles that old man Talltree had. Joeson smiled and said he still didn't know what he meant. He told Joeson that in medical terms he had something called "hemorrhoids" and that in his language he had a pain in his rear in.

Joeson was picked up and carried back home for the first few weeks by Doc Waters. Finally he had learned his own way and Amanda talked

Rob into letting him ride on his own. Because of him being a slave he always had to carry papers with him at all times stating who he was, who he belonged to, where he was going and where he was returning from.

Doc Waters had his hands full doctoring folks and didn't have time to make up his medicines. Joeson began making all of the medicines and remedies. People were beginning to over crowd his office just for his cures and Doc began to recognize the fact that Joeson had learned the fine art of medicine making and was an expert at it and now it was time to let him move on to bigger and better things.

Town folks and plantation owners were bringing their field hands in for all sorts of medical care. Joeson asked Doc Waters why not let him help handle the slave and field folk out in the back room while he handled the town folk. Doc disregarded and disagreed with the boy and paid little attention to what had been said.

Annabell brought over lunch and noticed the burdensome crowd and suggested he let Joeson give him a hand. He still tried to hold on to his stand but still found himself up a ladder. She reminded him why the boy was there to begin with and why they had a house full of new furniture and more to come.

After many days of being stormed to death a plantation owner came in with a large crowd of slaves and asked him why didn't he let the slave boy help if he knew how. He finally gave in and was sorry that he hadn't done it sooner because it was the smoothest day he had had in many long weeks. He went home that night and

told his wife that he felt like he had another
doctor in the office helping him.

Every day he would come to work and begin by
treating folks and letting them buy the little
bottles of medicine that he had already made
up. Once when no one was around a white lady by
the name of Miss Sara Lee Hawkins came in and
secretly let Joeson treat her and afterward
she gave him three gold pieces and told him to
just keep his mouth shut. He had learned the
trade well and could do everything Doc Waters
could do so he thought until a white lady came
by one morning with a back pain and the doctor
was out doing house calls.

Joeson offered to help her but the woman
reminded him he was still black and he still
was nothin but a slave servant and he could
be hung for even looking at her say nothin
about trying to touch a fine white lady like
herself. She told him that if he knew what she
know that he had better keep his doctoring
to animals, Indians and a few of them dumb
old slaves like himself. She walked out and
slammed the door in a rage saying to herself
that she ought to go tell her husband.

She was leaving just as Doc Waters came up
with his bag in his hand. He bid good day to
Miss Townslow and asked how your husband was
doing. She said he was doing just fine but she
thought she ought to tell him not to leave
that boy he got in your office alone anymore.

Doc invited her inside to tell him what she
was referring to. She said he thought he could
treat respectful white folk and handle them
like he handled them animals and other slaves.
Doc said he could see what the problem was and

assured her that when she left he would give that boy the thrashing of his life. She said she would certainly appreciate it because if he didn't he might come back sometimes from his rounds and find that boy dead from being lynched.

Doc Waters took time to explain the do's and don'ts to Joeson. Joeson said he already knew and all he did was ask that lady if she wanted him to help her and she went and got mad but he was sorry and next time he wouldn't say anything. Doc also asked Joeson to stop saying I's so much and start saying I when he was talking. Joeson agreed. He then said 'Now go on back to your office in the back, Doc Joeson. Joeson stopped in his tracks and asked Doc Waters what he had called him. Doc told him he had heard right, he called him Doc Joeson and from now on that was going to be his new.

He told him he had proven to him that he could really doctor folks and he was now officially giving him the title of doctor. Joeson was so happy that he just kept saying, "I'm a doctor; now I'm a doctor, just wait till I get back home and tell Ma and Pa."

He said no, he was going to tell Ms. Amanda and Master Henry first. He didn't know who he was going to tell first, he just had to tell somebody that his dream had come true, it had come true. Thank the Lawd, thank the Lawd, I am a doctor, he kept telling himself.

Doc Waters told him that now that he was Doc Joeson, he wanted to teach him one more thing. Joeson said, "Anything Doc Waters, anything!" Doc Waters said he had to try and teach him

how to read and write but that he had to keep
quiet about it and last of all he was going to
teach him how to use proper language because he
didn't know most of the folks that came there
leave saying behind his back that they didn't
know what he was saying half of the time.

Joeson shared with Doc Waters that he loved
him and thanked him. Doc thanked him for what
he had said and told him that he had made his
day because he needed that.

Day after day Joeson would come home and
tell his folks what he had learned different.
Doc Waters had great faith and confidence in
his new office helper until the day one of
the young slave girls went into labor. Joeson
watched and saw a child being born for his
first time and he became faint and sick.

As they were headed back to the office
Doc Waters had become very angry with Joeson
because he had gotten sick during the delivery.
He asked him what was wrong with him, hadn't
he ever seen a child been born before. He told
him he was a doctor now and not a wet nosed
kid and that if he did it again he was going
to make him stay at home and he would just
continue doing the doctoring alone. Joeson
stopped him and told him that he had never
seen a child being born before.

Doc Waters apologized for fussing at him
because he guessed he could understand it
some since it was the first time he had seen
a child being delivered after all he got a
little sick himself the first time and a few
times after that and he was sorry he got so
upset but if they didn't get no babies to
deliver then they eventually won't have any

folks to work on. Then he asked Joeson what he didn't understand about that. Joeson said the thing he didn't understand was about the babies. Doc Waters slowed down his carriage and pulled it to the side of the road and he looked strangely and confused into Joeson's face and questioned him softly about what he meant about not understanding about babies.

Joeson said he didn't understand where they came from. How something that big got inside of that slave gal in the first place. Waters began to laugh said to Joeson did he mean to tell him that he had made him an official doctor and he didn't even know where babies came from. He laughed harder and harder and said no wonder he got sick. Joeson asked him what was so funny. He wanted to know if it was something he said. Doc Waters kept right on laughing and said just wait until he got home and told his missies and he just couldn't wait to tell Old Rob and Amanda. Joeson wanted to know what was so funny because Doc Waters had never told him anything about making babies.

That afternoon Joeson came home and was telling his Ma and Pa what had happened that day and what Doc Waters had begun laughing about. After hearing his story they both began to laugh some and said that their son had made both of his parents as proud as they could ever be because he had become a fine doctor but . . . he didn't even know where babies came from.

His pa took him for a little walk outside and they both sat down under an old apple tree and his pa told him he was never going to be a fine doctor like he wanted until he knew more things but his parents were awfully proud of him anyway. His paw said he didn't know it all but he could at least tell him about the birds and the bees and where babies came from. After he told him, Joeson laughed all the way back home.

16

Homemade Moonshine

When Kate saw Doc Waters at the door, she bids him with a warm:

"Well how ya do there Doc Waters?"

"Why I'm just fine there, Kate. How ya and your Old man Joe?"

"We's doin just fine. Can Is takes ya hat and coat and hang um,sir?"

"Sure don't mind if ya do. Mr. Henry round any where's?"

"No sir hems been gone sense early this morning sir but Ms. Amanda's here sir, do ya wants us ta go fetch her fo ya sir?"

"Sure would if ya don't mind."

"Comes in here sir and have a seat in da parlor while Kate fetches her fo ya sir! Cans I's gets ya some-on ta drink or eat sir whiles ya waiting sir."

"I would like a little drink if ya got it!"

"Sho we's do sir, do ya wants tea or coffee sir?"

"Oh, neither Joe I need somethin strong ta dink . . . if ya know what I mean."

"Oh! Yes sir us got what ya wants alright!"

Old Joe goes and brings out a brown jug and pulls the cork and pours the doctor a big glass full. He takes a smell and says,

"That's shine ain't it?"

He takes a drink and says,

"My, my ain't that good."

He wiped his mouth and finished up the glass and began to laugh and said,

"Man I wish I knew where he bought that at and I would buy a few jugs of that fo myself."

"Well sir I's knows hems buy some of hem's liquor but hem's makes hem's own shine."

Doc Waters begins ta smile and says,

"Did ya just say that Mister Henry makes his own shine?"

"Why, hello there Ms. Amanda. How ya doing?"

"Just find Doc How's Ms. Annabel doing?"

"She's doing just fine. Old Joe here dun told me ya husband dun been gone now sense early this morning and I sho do wish he was here so I could see hem and have a little talk with hem."

"Yea Doc, here lately he leaves out pretty early everyday now and don't get back until late this evening. Is there anything I can do fo ya Doc?"

"Well maybe but I don't rightly know. Ya see I been missing Doc Joeson coming ta my office everyday lately and I was wondering what had happened?"

"What ya mean what's happened Doc?" "Joeson told us ya didn't want his help anymore!"

"Why did he say that, Miss Henry?"

"He said your white helper, Franklin, told hem ya had said that ya didn't need hem any more, and that he had done enough after he saved that child in da town's school yard and he even said ya had made some nasty remarks bout hem going back ta da cotton fields and picking cotton and never coming back cause he wasn't welcomed there anymore."

"Well Ms. Henry I never told Franklin ta tell Joeson no such thing."

"Well I just wonder then Doc Waters why Franklin told Joeson that then?"

"Well now Mrs. Henry ta tell ya da truth bout things I knew fo a fact da Franklin never did care that much fo Joeson anyhow Ms. Henry and ya know why."

"Well Doc Waters, did Franklin say anything ta ya bout Joeson or why he never came back or anything or something maybe ya can recall?"

"Well Ms. Henry yea he did, I can recollect Franklin telling me one morning after I returned back from an errand that Joeson had come ta da office and he left and said he had asked Franklin ta tell me he was sick and tired of me and he wasn't ever coming back again but Franklin never told me why Joeson said such a thing as that though."

179

"Well Doc did ya really believe Joeson had said that?"

"Come ta think of it Amanda at da time I did have mixed emotions bout it cause I do have ta admit I was running rail pretty hard sometimes on po Joeson but I, do care fo da boy though."

"Well then now Doc Waters, if what you're saying is true, ya should have come and told us and hem sooner, cause he told us he didn't ever want ta go back."

"Well, Ms. Henry despite how things might have looked at times I always knew Joeson was da best helper I ever had and I really knew he didn't kill that man on that operating table too because when I fust saw da needle work I knew right off hand who had did what and I guess I should have spoke up fo Joeson but I didn't. Ms. Henry, I guess I'm trying ta say I'm sorry if I ever wronged da boy anyways."

"Oh, Doc now ain't no cause fo all of that cause we all slip up at times and ain't none of us perfect."

"Yea I know Ms. Henry, but my conscious just won't let me sleep good at night lately and that's why I got ta face up and say I'm sorry!"

"Doc, tell me man, why did ya wait so long ta come see us or say something?"

"Well da truth is Ms. Henry I was a bit ashamed of how I had acted and what I had done."

"Well Doc Waters we had been wondering why ya never came by and when ya told Joeson ta tell

us not ta bring any more furniture we just
figured ya already had enough or ya wanted ta
get rid of Joeson and when he came and told us
what we thought ya had said, we told Joeson ta
just stay here and doctor our slaves. Since
that incident at da playground, other ranchers
and plantation owners been bringing their sick
slaves and animals out here and getting them
doctored on by Joeson."

"Oh, they are! (looking very upset and
surprised) Well, then that explains why my
business has gone down so much lately."

"What ya talkin' bout Doc Waters."

"Well ya see Ms. Henry, Joeson has been gone
now fo over four months and fo that period
of time I have been losing customers like
mad and now I seldom get any more slave
patients or any type of animals in my office
anymore and I sho do need hem ta come back
real bad like, if ya know what I mean."

"Well I'm so very sorry fo your business Doc,
but my husband dun gone and put hem an office
together out here on our place out back and
he works out there every day . . . , anyhow
Joeson told us he was scared sometimes fo his
life sometimes being with ya in town and now
he ain't scared of nothin out here."

"Well Miss Henry I guess I should do da right
thing and be glad fo da boy but I sho miss
hem and if it would be any constellation
ta hem, I want hem ta know that I dun gone
and got rid of old worthless Franklin cause
I can't afford ta pay hem anymore cause my
business dun got so bad and he didn't know
nothin bout doctoring folks no how. I tell

ya what if ya would let Joeson come back I'm sure I would find it in my heart ta even pay hem a mite ever now and then."

"Well Doc Waters, as I was saying, I'm so sorry ta hear that bout your doctoring business but . . . . Oh, look here comes Rob now."

Rob and Doc Waters sat in the parlor and they discussed da same matter Amanda had already told the good doctor and he saw that he was getting nowhere and he finally gives in and said,

"Well Rob if ya won't let hem come back, all I can do is wish hem well and if there is anything I can ever do fo da boy, just ask me."

Doc Waters looked at Rob with a half grin on his face and said,

"Rob if I ask ya something, ya wouldn't get mad at me would ya?"

"Well, I can't say that Doc, fust let me hear what ya gonna ask me."

"Ya see Rob, fust can't nobody hear me, can they?"

"No I don't recon nobody can hear ya Doc, but ta make sure I'll go close da door."

"Befo ya close da door Mr. Henry, do ya mind if I have another drink of that good tasting brew your house boy Old Joe gave me a little while ago?"

"What ya talking bout Doc Waters?"

"A he-he, ya know Rob some more of that good tasting shine."

Rob looked at Doc Waters and began to laugh then he went and got a jug of shine and two glasses to drink from and closed the door.

Both men began to drink and talk of old times
Doc said

"Mr. Henry, tell me man, where in da world
do ya buy this smooth tasting brew from?"
Rob smiled and said,
"Now Doc ya meddling ain't ya and why ya want
ta know anyhow?"

"Well ya see here Mr. Henry, it's like this;
when I make up a batch of my medicine I
always use whiskey and liquor and other
stuff and I have ta mix-um up together."
"Well tell me then Doc, what's that got ta
do with where I gets my liquor from (as he
smiled)?"

"Well Rob ta tell ya da truth, it costs
me a lots of money ta buy good liquor and
whiskey ta make stuff out of and if I could
make my own it sure would help my billfold
a lots."

"Doc Waters are ya telling me and asking
me what I think ya are?" "Why what's that Mr.
Henry?"

"Oh, come on now Doc, I just bet ya asked
Old Joe befo I came home where this shine came
from didn't ya?"

"Well it did sort of slip out of my mouth
Rob."

"And did Old Joe kind of let it slip out of
his mouth where I got it from?"

"Well now, he sort of did but ya know I
really didn't believe hem."

"What didn't ya believe Doc?"

"A he-he "I didn't believe hem when he said
ya made your own shine (A-he-he-he)."

"Ok now Doc ya know; tell me what ya got in
mind?"

"Well let's see here all I got in mind is would ya show me how ta make it, just fo medicine making only though and I give ya my promise and my solemn word I, never would drink non myself."

"Doc do ya have a paper and pencil handy in your pocket?"

"I show do Rob."

"Well write this down then; four big bags of sugar."

"How big Rob, five pound bags or ten pound bags?"

"No man I mean four one hundred pound bags each; one five pound sack of yeast, a barrel of barley and a barrel of crushed corn or corn mash and if ya want a real mellow taste get a tub of peaches or apricots or some kind of fruit that ya like da best."

"Now Mr. Henry just what in tar nations I'm supposed ta do with da likings of all that stuff man?"

"Well Doc ya just bring all that there stuff ya dun put own your paper there and bring it all in a wagon this weekend, and make sure your wife and mine don't catch ya and I'll show ya!"

"Mr. Henry I tell ya what man ya know ya sho is something else. Tell me Mr. Henry, do ya know how ta make wines and beer and all of that there kind of stuff?"

"Sure I do Doc, Don't ya know? I thought everybody here and bout's know how ta make that little old stuff."

"Well I tell ya what Mr. Henry, I'm afraid you're wrong cause I certainly don't."

"*Ya mean ta tell me ya a doctor and don't even know how ta make wine or beer; man I see I got a lots of teaching ta teach ya.*"

"*Well Mr. Henry I'm sho here ta learn.*"

"*I tell ya what Doc, since ya like my shine so much, I'm going ta go an fetch ya and me a jar of wine I made last fall and a jar of beer and let ya see how ya like them.*"

They were already drinking from a half gallon jug of shine and Rob returned back with two quart jars of his delightful brews. One was bubbling and fizzling full of good homemade beer and da other was Mother Nature's best tasting wine.

"*Here Doc, have yourself a big glass of this.*"

"*Why what in da world is that stuff there Mr. Henry?*" *It's all foamy looking on da top like my wives wash water when she does our washing on her scrub board or that bubble bath stuff she's always bathing herself with; and look, it's all purple like ain't it.*"

Rob took the seal off of the top and poured him and Waters a big heaping glass full and he said, "*Here man stop yacking so darn much man and just heave up da glass and drink man, good Lawd.*"

Waters picked up the glass with a dismayed look on his face before he tasted the fine brew. After the sweet taste touched his dried and thirsty tongue, he just couldn't seem to put the glass down and when it was emptied a couple of times he put out his glass for more, more, more.

"Umm, umm ain't that good, my Lawd, my Lawd that really do hit da spot don't it, man that stuffs made, bottled and dun been sent straight from heaven ain't it! Ya don't have ta tell me . . . either, man that's Scubney dime wine ain't it. Man it sho is good" (hic-up) . . . can I have another (hic-up, hic-up).glass (ah-ah-he-he)?"

"Sure ya can Doc, just knock yourself out but fust ya ain't even tried any of my beer yet and if ya think that shine and wines good, jest ya wait till you've tried this good homemade beer I got fo ya."

"Now Rob (Ah-he-he-he) don't fill my glass so full man (hiccup) (burp) this time ya gonna, gonna gonna (burp)(hic-up)be done gone and got me (burp, burp, burp) drunk. Woo woo my head, my head, Lawd my po head feels as light as a feather from a duck dawn pillow (burp, burp) (hic-up) hee heee Rob or Mr. Henry (hic-up) tell me some-on (hic-up, hic-up) is it hot in here too. This some sho nuff good beer ain't it (burp, burp, burrppp) (he-he-he) how ya make this (S t u f f) (hic-up) (burp, burp)."

"Go on, drink da rest of that jar fust Doc befo I tell ya. I got ta get ya some of my rice wine fust and let ya have a sip then I'll tell ya."

Rob returned back with the jar of rice wine and said, *"Well Doc, I'm sorry it took so long fo me ta come back cause what I dun was I had hid it from myself and I see ya dun gone and finished and polished off da rest of that shine, wine and beer. Hey Doc, Doc, Doc"*

Well I'll be, he dun gone and fell asleep in that rocking chair there with his eyes wide opened. I wonder what happened that short while that I was gone. A-he-he-he!

17
Epidemic

I recall when I was asked to fetch Joeson so Doc Waters could talk to him a spell about a sickness that was going on about town. When I came back with Joeson, Doc Waters began to talk to him about the sickness that Doctor called an epidemic. Everyone asked Doc Waters just what is an epidemic? He said an epidemic is a sickness that a whole bunch of folks come down with and most of them die from it.

When it first started to get a hold on a body they act just like they got morning sickness but then it gets a lot worst. They get a real high fever and then they get the shakes and later on they just up and die. Joeson wanted to know if men and women get this ailment and if little children get it too? Doc Waters said that anybody could get it. Folks everywhere were dying like flies and nobody knew what to do about it. Doc told Miss Henry that he ain't never seen no critters sick from it but he sure had been waiting on lots and lots of sick folks in and about town.

There wasn't any cure or treatment. The Doc would tell people to boil all of the ailing folk's clothes and bedding and everything they touch. Folks needed to make real sure to boil the water and maybe even boil the milk befo they drank it. People thought the Doc had gone too far.

They said that even in the good book, the Lawd promised us milk and honey. Ain't no sickness ever got in no milk before. They asked if maybe they should boil their honey too. Doc said you never can tell what them little germ critters and things might get into.

Doc got to callin' on his schooling when he learned that flies, bugs and insects can carry lots of sickening stuff at times. Everybody was told they might need to put dirt into all of the out houses and clean up all of the animal stalls, chicken coops and pour dirt on all of the rough and bad places and out in the pastures, too.

Over thirty towns' folks died and most of them were grown and out in the plantations and forty more had died in other places and many more were sick from it. The young folks are suffering like everything and dozens of then dying and dead. Mr. and Mrs. Henry had buried eight or nine folks in one week alone and even two of them were white. One was the wife of one of the row masters and the other was his youngest son.

Ms. Henry didn't really know what they died from, all she could tell Doc was that they were yelling something bout their heads were bothering them something terrible and they all just up and died out in the fields. Doc kept asking questions trying to figure out what was making them sick. He thought they had a bad case of the dysentery.

The three men went for a walk through the camp to see for themselves. Three more slaves were infected before the week had ended; many others had become sick and three more young children died.

One of the children that had become sick of the epidemic had gotten cured. The child's mother had seen this type of sickness many years before and she knew the cure. She made an herbal tea from the bark of the albino bush and berries of the swine weeds bush. She told her fellow slave friends and they and their children lived. She told Joeson the cure and he began making the cure and giving it to the other plantation owners.

Workers in the fields were down to a minimum and on all plantations and farms people were still dying like flies. Doc Waters had his hands full trying to control this serious disaster. Many were fleeing the town and burning their houses, many of the fires had leaped onto and into many fields and wooded areas. The third month and second week of this problem Old Joe, Joeson's pa, also died. He did not get the tea in time to cure him.

Just as rain has no respect of person it wets whoever it hits, slaves and slave masters alike were all equally crying and dying at the same time. Doc Waters had to hurry and rehire Franklin. News of the herbal tea had not leaked out to Doc Waters. The slaves on the Henry plantation were but almost recovered.

Unable to visit the Henry plantation himself, Waters sent Franklin over to see how the Henrys were fairing. During the visit, Joeson told Franklin he had not found the cause of the epidemic but a slave had found the cure. Franklin never told Doc Waters that Joeson had told him the cure. Doc Waters also died of the epidemic. Shortly after his death, the towns' folks made Franklin their new doctor. Franklin had convinced everyone that he had found the cure for the epidemic by making an herbal tea.

The epidemic had finally gone and almost all of the plantations and farms were back in order again. Recovery was costly and many had loved ones who had died and many homes had been burned and stores had gone out of business. Amanda and Kate both seemed to be still ailing from something. Rob had Joeson and Luanna the old slave woman to make more of the herbal tea. Amanda, Kate and the other slaves were given large doses to drink.

Another epidemic was about to start but no one was aware. However, this time folks won't be crying they will be laughing and rejoicing. All of the town folks, plantation and farm owners were drinking the tea now for just in case of. It was a common place thing to see a jug or two in every house and cabin.

During the time of the highlight of the crises, even before old Franklin had learned the cure, a rich plantation owner came and bought some of Joeson's tea and saved the lives of his wife and children. The man came one afternoon and thanked Joeson for saving his family. Before he left he asked Joeson was there any way he could ever repay him.

Joeson told the man that it wasn't him that found the cure. The man wanted to know who it was if it wasn't him. Joeson told him it was one of the old slave women out in the fields. Mr. Cleavers asked Rob and Amanda could he see and talk to this woman. Rob got one of his field workers to go get her.

She came up to the big house with a rather confused look on her face and inquired why Master Rob Henry wanted her. She began to apologize if she had done something wrong. He assured her that she hadn't done anything wrong as he tried to calm her down. She insisted on knowing why he had called for her. She was afraid that maybe he was getting ready to sell her off.

He told her to be quiet a moment so he could tell her what he called her for. She told him of a time when a Master called her up to his house and it was for a whipping. Amanda assured her that she didn't have nothin to worry about because nobody was gonna whip her.

The man asked Luanna how she knew about the tea. She told him that she had seen this type of epidemic before when she was a young lady and one of her children had died from it. The man wanted to know what the tea was made from but Rob and Amanda refused to let Joeson and Luanna tell. Mr. Cleavers offered to buy Luanna but Rob refused to sell her.

Cleavers finally asked Luanna was there anything he could do to ever repay her. She said yes there was. She said she didn't want to say because she was still afraid of receiving a whipping. Again, Rob and Amanda assured her that she was not going to get a whipping. She said she wanted all her children set free as she began to cry.

Master Henry told her she knew good and well he wasn't gonna do nothin like that. Cleavers told him to just wait because he had an idea. Master Henry asked to hear more. Cleavers said if Master Henry could sell her family to him. Master Henry told Cleaver that she had over nine family members living out here and even if he did sell them it would cost over ten thousand dollars and ain't nobody in their right mind would fork over that much money for a hand full of no count slaves.

Mr. Cleaver said he wouldn't say that then turned to Miss Luanna and asked again if she said her whole family. She told him indeed she did. He went on to tell Master Henry that he couldn't resist the woman's request since she was the cause of his family being alive.

He asked Master Rob how much for the whole lot. Master Henry tried to jack the price up to twelve thousand dollars but Cleavers told him he recollected him saying ten thousand but he offered him twenty for the whole lot.

Master Rob reminded Mr. Cleavers that he was only paying for her children and grandchildren because Luanna was not for sale. Mr. Cleavers asked Mr. Henry if he would let her go if he paid twenty-five. Master Rob said no way, not even for a million dollars. Cleavers admitted that Mr. Henry drove a hard bargain but he would be by the next day to pick up his property and

to make sure they were all ready and he'd have
a draft made unless he wanted cash money.

Two days later Cleavers arrived and took off
with his newly purchased property. Cleavers
offered ten thousand dollars for Mother Luanna
but Rob still refused. Before slaves are sold
off they were always allowed to say good bye
to their loved ones. Many tears fell during
the good bye session. Luanna cried as the
wagons drove off.

Amanda began to cry for her and ran to her
husband's arms and begged Rob to please let her
go, she pleaded with Mister Rob please to let
that poor woman go free. All he said was no,
not yet. Amanda had asked Luanna the afternoon
when Cleavers first came to thank her if any
of their plantation workers had been with any
of the women on their plantation.

Amanda later learned from Luanna that there
had been numerous times when the white men
workers had forced themselves and laid with
the slave girls and women. Luanna told Ms.
Amanda that's why there were so many light
looking slave children around. Amanda asked
was her husband ever with any of them. Luanna
lied when she said no. Amanda asked Rob to
fire them, he said he would, but he never did.
Luanna was sent back to the fields. She cried
bitterly for her children. One afternoon Rob
came home and said he was going out for an
afternoon ride. A man came to Luanna's cabin
and took her for a ride. She ended up far out
in the woods and several white men met them
and Rob was with them. She was asked why she
told what she had told. They all held her and
laid with her, tied her to a tree and whipped

her. She confessed telling but said she didn't tell on Master Henry. She was taken back home and turned loose and went back to the fields the next day.

Two weeks had passed and Amanda still was feeling poorly and she had gone into town to see how her dead friend's wife was doing. While she was gone over to Annabell's house Rob came home for lunch and went upstairs for a short nap. He yelled and told me to go fetch Luanna for him. Luanna came up to his house and climbed the stairs. She knocked on the door and he told her to come in.

He told her to close the door. Rob opened the door and looked down the stairs and told Kate to go for a long walk and stay for a while. She did what he said but couldn't help wondering what that man was gonna do to that poor woman. Kate wished Ms. Amanda would hurry up and come home.

He asked Luanna what he had to do to keep her from crying so much out in the fields. He said he was sick and tired of it and he was going to teach her a lesson and told her to go get over on his bed. He then told her to take her clothes off. She began to cry and say that she would do anything he said.

He laid with her and told her she better not tell. She put her torn clothing back on and he could hear that Amanda had come back home. Kate was back in the house and knew what was going on. Kate told Amanda that Rob was upstairs asleep and he wanted her to wake him up in a few minutes. She said okay that she would go wake him up.

Rob came to the door of his room and looked down the stairs and said hi to Ms. Amanda and that he had heard her come inside. She asked him why he was sleeping that time of day because he had never napped at that time of day before. He lied and said he was just tired and changed the subject. He asked her what all she bought.

She said just a few hats and gowns. She asked him to go get her things off of the wagon. He came down the stairs and kissed her. She asked him why he was so smelly and she almost said he smelt like a slave woman or something. He tried convincing her that she was imagining things. They both left to fetch the packages and I hurried to let Luanna out the side door.

The next morning when Master Rob and I were alone in the kitchen and Amanda is upstairs in bed he thanked Kate for the day before. I kept insisting that I needed to talk to Master Rob but he was not trying to hear me until I told him about the bloody sheets that I had taken off the bed and put into the closet.

Kate said he was horrified to learn that I only had time to throw them in the closet. I was quite certain that Amanda would be going into the closet with her new purchases. Rob was really, really nervous and upset with me. I told him I was only trying to help.

Amanda had a habit of getting up sometimes and going to the closet to get fresh sheets to put on the bed. Rob was clearly in a jam and needed to be bailed out again. I agreed to help him out again but to show his gratitude, he would have to let the old woman, Luanna go

free. Rob told me that I knew good and well
why he couldn't do that. He told me that Mr.
Cleavers didn't want to buy that woman because
of what she did for him it was because she
knew the secret to making that herbal tea.

I told him that might be right but what
about her, the poor woman's got feelings like
anybody else. She wanted so bad to be with her
children and grandchildren. I told him that
her heart was broken and he didn't understand
because his heart hadn't ever been broken
before and that's why the poor woman cries so
much. I pleaded with him that they had done
enough to that poor woman. He finally gave in
and agreed to let her go if I would explain
what I meant about they had done enough to
her.

Word had gotten around about what you fine
white men folk did to her out yonder in the
wood is what I told him. Once I began to cry
Master Rob said he promised to let her go
just tell him the rest. Right about then,
Ms. Amanda began to yell from upstairs for
Rob to come look at what she found hidden in
the closet when she was going to change the
sheets. Before I would save him, I made him
swear again that he would free Luanna. He went
upstairs and offered Ms. Amanda her breakfast
and asked what on earth she was raving about.
I knocked on the door before she can answer.
She asked what or who it was.

I answered and said it was time for me to
come take out the sheets and wash them. With
those sheets in her hand she asked me if I
knew where the blood came from that was on the
sheets.

I replied that I knew and forgot to tell her yesterday that I bumped my nose and it started bleeding after I had taken them off of the bed. I apologized and Ms. Amanda just told me to try to be more careful next time. He said that if the blood didn't come out that I was going to get a whipping. Ms. Amanda told him that he knew good and well that he wasn't gonna do no such thing.

Rob could see that me and Amanda were still ailing from something but what he couldn't rightly put his finger on. The next few days we both began to complain more of having the fever, shakes, and extreme pain in our lower backs. Rob went to fetch Doc Franklin, however he was gone from his office so Rob went to the saloon for a little drink and a game or two of cards.

He returned back at Franklin's office before he left town and the Doc still had not returned. In the town saloon Rob learned from other men that their wives also were ailing from lower back pains. One old man had suggested that some other type of sickness might be going around because many women were complaining of the same thing.

The old pop said it might be the same killer he had seen back in the twenties when he was just a kid. He said all of his sisters and ma began having bad back pains and was hot and cold and a week or two later they all died.

Rob rode back home but he was becoming very worried for his wife's welfare. As he entered the plantation many of his slave men were speaking to him and asking him how he was doing. He would say fine and how about them.

They told him they were fine but their women were ailing some. He asked them what seemed to be the problem. Most would say their wives were complaining of back pains. He got up to his house and a servant met him and took his horse and carried it to the barn.

Before the servant took his horse he said, "Congratulations, Master sir." Mr. Henry looked somewhat confused at what was just said to him, but he still politely said okay. He went inside the house and saw Annabell, Doc Waters' widow and many other town folks. He had been gone for almost all of the day but he still wondered why so many folks were there.

Deacon Clarence greeted him and asked him how he was doing and acknowledged it had been a long time since he last saw him. He said he was doing just fine, now he wanted to know what was going on wrong. Rob even saw the town undertaker and his wife and cold chills began to run up and down his spine. He knew that the only time he ever saw those two monsters is after a birth or death.

Clarence told Master Henry to calm down and he thought that he ought to go sit down, while he told him what was going on and he thought he ought to be the one to tell him what done happened to his wife since the town preacher is out of town for a spell.

Rob demanded to know what he was talking about. Just then the undertaker and his wife came up smiling. Rob yelled he wanted to know what was going on. He ran up the stairs to his bedroom and saw some of his slave women making up his bed but his wife was not around nowhere.

He questioned the slave women about where his wife was. They said they didn't know and that some white folk downstairs came and took her to another room. Rob yelled out that somebody better tell him something. Everybody told Master Rob to calm down a bit before he wake up the children.

From the distance, Ms. Amanda told him he was being too loud and asked her where she was. He said it sounded like a baby was crying in their guest chamber bedroom. He said everybody knew he didn't like for no children to be in their guest bedroom. He said that if he found any of them slave children playing in their guest chamber that he was going to whip their . . .

He got to the chamber door and opened it and there laid Amanda smiling at him. He asked what was wrong because the folks in the house had scared him nearly half blind and that the old undertaker . . . . Amanda told Rob to be quiet she loved him too. He asked Ms. Amanda who she had crying under the cover with her. He told her that she better not have taken one of the slaves children again be trying to nurture it and pretending to be a mother here again.

She told him before she turned back the cover and to let him see, he had to first promise not to get mad. He told Amanda okay, he promised. She pulled back the patched quilt and there laid two of the most darling looking set of twins Rob had ever seen. He smiled and said they were beautiful and whose children were they.

She asked him whose children he thought they
were? Rob questioned if she meant to tell him
that they belonged to him. She said yes, that
the twins were his. She told him to see their
first born twins, a boy and a girl. The girl
was crying but her brother was sound asleep.

Deacon Clearance came to the door and saw
Rob weak in the knees and told him to sit
down. The undertaker took him a glass of water
and told him to take a sip. They all began to
laugh and rejoice, including Rob.

Rob finally realized his wife had been in
the family way but never told him. The medicine
Joeson was giving everyone to drink had caused
her babies to come early. Mother Luanna forgot
to tell folks that her brew was also used as
a fertility drink as well as a cure for many
sicknesses.

Joeson delivered two or three babies a week
now fo a few weeks. When Rob had went for the
doctor in town, he later learned he was gone
because he was out delivering babies. Roberta
and Robert were the names given to the twins.
Rob was tickled pink.

I had drunk many glasses of the tea but
it seemed that something else was causing me
to ail. Seven days after the twin's birth my
ailment began to concern my son more and more.
Amanda had an idea what was wrong with me
but told Joeson maybe I was mourning my dead
husband in a strange way.

Mother Luanna was allowed to take care of the
big house while I was feeling poorly because
she was wise in her years. She knew and could
see things even the doctor couldn't figure.

When mother Luanna first saw me lying in bed she didn't look sadly at me but she smiled and told me she understood and that it would be soon. Joeson became very scared and was going to give me more of the tea but Mother Luanna told him not to because I had had enough.

Mother Luanna passed by my shack before she went up to the big house and hurried up to Ms. Amanda's room one morning and told Master and Ms. Amanda come quick because I was getting sicker. Amanda told her to go get Joeson. He hurried from out back and Amanda met them out at my cabin.

Joeson came to my side and was giving me some of the tea. Amanda and Luanna had come inside and told Joeson to leave the room but he refused. Mother Luanna was angry with Joeson because she had asked him not to give her any more of the tea because of what it could cause.

Joeson questioned the Mother about why she was angry with him. She and Amanda smiled but Amanda answered Joeson and said, Now boy don't you know where babies come from? Joeson refrained yes he did and why was she asking? Amanda told Mother Luanna to go on and tell him, it was obvious to her that this doctor didn't have the faintest. Joeson was confused. Mother Luanna told Joeson that I was in the family way and it was not time for me to have my baby yet but that tea was making my child be born too fast and if it came now it would die.

The next day my baby had to come but it died after the delivery. The child looked just like old Joe. It was a boy she named him Joesrealson before they buried it. Joeson wondered why I chose that name instead of Joeson just like his name.

When all of the epidemics were settled down and Amanda was able to return back to church, Pastor Larson preached a good message one morning about someone who had to die so others could be born. Because folks believed the tea was the cause of so many babies being born, it had become the number one gift at weddings and old folks were secretly buying it by the jugs and barrels. The tea helped Joeson to learn a great lesson. Sometimes a doctor's medicines can start and save lives but sometimes sorry to say it can also take life too.

18

Miss Sara Lee Hawkins

Kate recalled the early twilight of the morning when she saw a lovely carriage being driven through the heart of town. The carriage was one of the finest money could buy. It had an overhead covering with tiny little tassels dangling down. The buggy was driven by an angelic looking elderly lady all dressed up in blue and lovely scarlet tapestry. The real lady, or should I say the owner of the coach, was sitting in the second seat of the coach with a lovely flower veiled hat that was slightly draped over her heart shaped face. The owner wore a red ruby stone with a slight chip in the bottom corner that was attached to a lovely chain necklace and her smell was of fine perfume and cinnamon.

As the coach entered the town all heads was turned. Almost everybody that was somebody knew the current owner and the original owner of this fine coach. It was Miss Hawkins, Miss

Sara Lee Hawkins. She was the granddaughter of the town's late church pastor. Her buggy still had the sign of the cross attached to it and her grandfather's name engraved on the side. The towns' church had given it to her grandfather on his twenty-fifth pastoral anniversary and it was willed to her after his death.

Reverend and Mrs. Hawkins had only one child together that lived and they gave her a biblical name, Mary Ruth. Mary Ruth grew up and had a daughter and she gave her a biblical first name Sara, with a second name, Lee. Now Sara was believed to be a very upstanding highly respected lady and loved by the young and old. When Sara Lee grew up she was very spoiled.

One Sunday morning before church service had begun, Reverend Hawkins announced that his daughter Ruth had left suddenly for a school out of state. A few months later she returned back with a little baby girl named Sara Lee. No one ever proclaimed to have ever seen the child's pa, so they pretended. Blushing, Ruth told the congregation that she had met up with her daughter's pa in the town at the out of state school and they soon got hitched. She told the saddest story of how before she could finish with her schooling he somehow mysteriously got killed on a cattle drive or hunting accident or something or the other so she just came back home. Most folk just looked the other way and said behind her back that they had noticed her belly beginning to rise before she left. She had only been gone for about four months before she came back.

When Mary Ruth came back with little Sara Lee the Sheriff's son looked awfully guilty every time he saw the child and so did Jonny James Eckers as well as and a few other young men in town. However, she was the preacher's daughter so no one ever said anything; she just went back to being the children's Sunday school teacher.

In the town and surrounding township, rumor was that Rev. Hawkins had a few outside children. There were about four or five little boys and girls that looked a lot like him, but he swore they were the work of one of his four other brothers that lived in town who lived loose lives. Before Rev. Hawkins had married his wife Tina, she had two sons already.

Rev. Hawkins was her only husband. They meet at a railroad construction company. William Hawkins was a spike driver for the Southern Railroad when he met Tina Colds. Tina was a cook and contractor for dynamite and high explosives for the railroad gang. She had both sons by her side when they first met. Three years after they met they had two sets of twins that died.

After five and a half years of courtship, traveling, and living together they both finally decided to settled down and get hitched. That fall, Mary Ruth was born. Their courtship was smooth but the beginning of their marriage was like a storm. William would get paid by the railroad and other odd jobs and spend most of his money on hard liquor, fast women, and gambling before he would get home.

Once, in a gambling dispute, William killed a man and he was sent to prison for life. Tina was a very pretty woman. Most men would have given their eye tooth to have been her man. Tina remembered the things her mother and grandmother had told her to do if she was ever in dire need of money. On the fourth year of William's prison sentence, Tina had another set of twins but they were a girl and a boy this time and sorry to say they both died of the fever before their fourth birthday.

William had been in prison for over seven years and made his parole on the grounds of good behavior. Shortly before his parole he began preaching and the warden just happened to have heard him and it was by faith that he got released.

Tina's mother had become rather old and frail but she helped to make ends meet the best she could while William was away. Shortly after his parole, Tina's mother died of a serious unexplainable cough and back ailment. The sons Tina had before she meet William turned out to be very fine, prosperous, and upstanding young men.

John Silver became a river boat captain and Jessie Coles became a mortician. Mary Ruth was a very tiresome child. Her mother had a hard time trying to raise her and her two older brothers. Tina did the best she could to raise three children alone.

Mary Ruth, Reverend and Mrs. Hawkins, all died and Sara Lee had hard times to come her way, but she still somehow continued to come to church faithfully. The bills and mortgages began to mount up and the church's congregation was small and most of the folks were only poor dirt farmers. They all did all they could to help but the wolves were continuously hounding at her door.

After much prayer and supplication, she said a happy and joyful little voice told her to start a little ranch. The voice told her and showed her how she could be loaded with money. She did what the voice had told her and sure enough she soon had loads and loads of money. Her ranch was not the ordinary type of ranch where you would see cowboys outside rounding up cattle and branding. One could be for sure that any time of day or night some cowboy would surely be there.

Her ranch was a girl's ranch or should I say a woman's ranch. Kate wouldn't say what some of the old nasty, nosey, and gossiping church women folk called it and you just wouldn't believe what they called poor Miss Sara Lee Hawkins. The kind voice that had spoken to this kind lady reminded her of how her poor dearly beloved mother had made a living when her father was away in prison and sometimes when he was out working on the railroad.

Tina said it was the only true way she knew of how to really make ends meet before she became the preacher's wife. Grandmother Colds had once told Sara that it had been a trade for women even at the beginning of time and during the time of the Lawd.

Any young girl or woman that had no place to go could always find shelter and a morsel of bread at Miss Sara Lee Hawkins' house. Some folks even swore that a few runaway slave girls and women had found refuse there. The women and girls there would plow and harvest their own crops and fields. They did their own branding and butchering of their own cattle and livestock. Often times, a few of the men folk around about town would help them with their plowing and such.

Some men folk had been rumored to have been seen bringing bags of food and whatever in and out. Some even claim that the women didn't totally except free labor and that charity was totally out of the question because they would pay the men folk for helping with the plowing and such, but we won't discuss how they were paid.

The town sheriff for some reason made it his business to do a security check on her ranch every afternoon before he went home. He made sure it was safe and had not come to any mischief. The mayor's wife caught him more than once or twice delivering hams and chickens, but of course you know that the mayor had a civil duty to take donations to the needy. He even carried over seven whole cut up cows and a hog; but the hog was just a little bitty one. Before he got married, Rev. Larson, the town's parson, was caught by the sheriff coming out of the ranch. The town's store keeper had brought over a goat, a big fat hog and a milk cow.

When the sheriff and the storekeeper questioned the parson about what he was doing and why was he out that late at night to bring gifts, he just said that while he was in his bed asleep a dream came to him and told him to share what he had with the poor and needy. They asked him why he was at that lady's bedside kneeling down with his pants pulled down. He said it was because he just had to have a private nightly prayer with her. Oh yes, he said, his pants just happened to have fallen down while he was kneeling to pray because his belt buckle broke loose.

The town's blacksmith ran a poultry farm and he made sure they had plenty of fresh eggs, chickens, turkeys and geese for Thanksgiving and Christmas. He had more than he and his family could ever eat or sell and his wife never did ask, so he just never did tell her.

The preacher was always preaching about when you give, you should do it in secret. The bartender watered down most of his drinks so he would take the leftovers and just donate it to the poor and needy ranch women. The saloon owner and his wife never did suspect anything, so just like the black smith he never said a word.

Usually the Mayor would carry over the little donations but the blacksmith, sheriff and bartender took over their own. The preacher made his own deliveries to but he tried to do it in secret, just like the good book said. Master Henry was just about the only man in town that had not had any bad rumors, but Amanda did question Rob a time or two about the smell of loud perfume and cinnamon when he would come home so late at night.

However, there was a certain missing horse that Amanda saw a certain young lady riding into town. She never told the town women because she knew it would cause rumors but she sure whipped and tried to beat old Rob's head.

The poor ladies at the ranch would take in washing and ironing for anyone who needed it done. Many of the town's women folk would have their fancy needle and sewing work done at Miss Sara Lee's ranch. Many of the women and young ladies would care for the town children when they were ailing. The ranch and cow hands would have their britches and shirts mended and their worn out knees and seats patched along with and a few other things taken care of.

Many of the women that came to have their sewing and such done were totally too blind to see what Miss Hawkins was really doing at her house. Some of the old gossiping women in town claimed the ranch was the cause of some kind of an itch that was going around. They had nothin or anyone to put it on so they put it on the ranch.

Many of the town folks were coming down with a rash on their hands, arms, feet and ankles and on their hidden private parts. Doc Waters said he was sure it wasn't poison ivy, thunder wood or shoe mack in the air and it might have been some sorts of measles that only ground folks got.

Doc Waters didn't know what the origin was so he just called the problem "It". After handling the folks with "It", Doc Waters came down with "It" and he gave "It" to his wife. Waters had his wife wondering if he was telling the truth or not on how he really caught "It". Children never seemed to be affected with this "It" rash and itch. The people that had "It" would complain of constantly itching and burning and having chills and fever but "It" only lasted a few weeks and then "It" just went away.

Because of the many different possibilities and the wide variety of "It", many women would stay clear of the ranch and they dared their husbands to ever go near the ranch (to keep them from temptation). Many of the church women had planned to burn Miss Sara Lee and her house with fire.

They would often complain to the Sheriff and ask him to run her out of town but he never did anything because he knew most of the men folk in town would run him out before they would see her run out. Her ranch had brought much money into town. It helped the town to grow tremendously. Miss Sara Lee had paid for the school pews and she had pledged to pay half of the teacher's salary and of course she gave very big in the church's offering plate

She paid more than a quarter of the sheriff's salary even though he was giving her back more than half of what he made. If anyone got burned out or got sick and couldn't make their way, she would always give them huge donations and a place to stay until they were able to get back on their feet. All of the town's kids just loved her. If any stranger or wearied traveler wondered into town and had no resting place, any child or even the Sheriff would direct them to her place of refuge to spend the night.

Her peppermints and rock candies just stole the hearts of the little children and old men at church and at school. The church's Sunday school attendance increased greatly after she began coming. Old and young men alike started to attend regularly just because of her presence.

Wives no longer had to complain to their men folk about being late for church meetings. When Miss Sara Lee would come to church every Sunday, she would insist that everybody at her ranch had to come with her. The town church had to be enlarged twice just because of this fine lady.

One morning a knock came on Doc Waters' office door. Franklin asked who was it as he went to the office door and opened it. There stood one of the loveliest ladies you ever did see. Franklin's eyes bugged and lit up like a candle as he drooled at the mouth as he spoke to her. Franklin eye balled her from her head down to her toes.

She asked if Doc Waters was around. Franklin told her no and asked whether or not she had heard the bad news that Doc Waters had been dead for over a month or more. He went on to tell her that he was the new town doctor.

She expressed her surprise to hear about Doc Waters and how that fine soft handed gentleman died. Franklin told her that it was some kind of epidemic that the old slaves were giving folks. She asked Franklin if he was around when Doc had the epidemic. Franklin admitted that he was. She then asked him why he didn't catch it and die. He told her he had found out the cure for it after Doc Waters had died.

The beautiful woman went on to say that if he was now the new town doctor, what happened to the black boy that used to care for the slave folk and animals? Franklin said he went back to picking cotton on Old Man Henry's Plantation and that some folks even said his Master allowed him to tend to his sick slaves on the plantation.

Franklin poked fun at that and started laughing thinking the lady was going to laugh with him. She said it was more of a laugh that

she just left from the Henry Plantation and
she recollected seeing that little old slave
boy and he was doing better than him. Now he
questioned her about what she meant by that
because there wasn't anything that boy can do
better than him.

She said she wouldn't say that because once
she came here late one afternoon and Doc Waters
and no other white folks were around and she
had been feeling so poorly until she just had
to let somebody do something for her and no one
was looking, so she just let him take care of
her. She rubbed his nose in just how good that
black boy knew how to doctor. He made her feel
better in a hurry. She found out for herself
why all of her black girls always asked her to
let them come and get him to check them out.

She said she never paid Waters for his
service because he never really did that good
of a job but she gave that boy not one silver
coin but three gold coins. Franklin got good
and mad and started yelling

She told him there was no need for carrying
on like that because she was only joshing
with him anyhow. She said she always heard
her dearly departed granddaddy, the Reverend
William Hawkins, say that laughter was a good
medicine. He asked her what she came there for
as he spit his tobacco into his spittoon.

She said she was coming by for her yearly
checkup. He asked her just what she wanted him
to check. She told him she wanted him to check
everywhere. He asked her name and she replied
Miss Sara Lee Hawkins to you.

He asked her again to make sure she said,
Miss Sara Lee Hawkins. She assured him that he

had heard correctly and asked if he had heard of her before. He replied that he had indeed heard of her but he wouldn't dare repeat what he heard. She goaded him to go ahead and tell her what he had heard. He said he didn't think he would say but he did have a question for her.

She told him to go ahead and tell her want he wanted to know. He asked her if she was the owner of that women's ranch out across from Turkey and Beehive Creeks. She said she sure was and asked him to tell the truth about whether he had ever wanted to come visit her ranch. He was embarrassed and went back to looking for his rubber gloves so he could get started with her checkup.

After Franklin came back with his gloves, Miss Sara Lee asked him if he would please come by her ranch and check out a couple of her girls that were feeling poorly. Franklin asked her what was wrong with the girls. She said she didn't rightly know but they said they had forgotten to drink their tea every morning. He asked what tea she was talking about. She said it was just an herbal tea. He wanted to know what kind of herbal tea it was. She told him it was a tea made from red pepper parts and the blossoms of this wild flower they found out in the woods.

He told her that it sounded like some kind of a witch's brew or the devil's drink. She told him not to go bad mouthing her girls. He asked her just what did the tea do for a body. She said it was a tea just for women folk. It made them feel good and they needed it for the type of work they did and that sometimes if they didn't take it as they been told to, they wouldn't feel good for months, bout nine months to be exact.

He told her he taught he knew what she meant. He said he thought it would be better if she brought your girls there for him to see them instead of him going to the ranch to see them. She told him that before she left she was going to do her best to make him change his mind. She went on to ask him if she brought over a couple of her girls for him to check, did he want her to bring him a taste of her tea. He asked her why he would want any of that witche's brew. She said it would prevent him from ever catching any type of disease.

Franklin tried to begin the examination but she complained of the roughness and coldness of the gloves and insisted that he take them off. He checked her all over as she had requested. He did the best a young doctor of his little experience could do. After finishing the examination Franklin was as red as a pumpkin' sweating and his hands and knees were shaking like a leaf because of the pay she had given him.

They both exited the examination room and there were a few older town folks waiting in the waiting room to see the doctor. They could hear Franklin telling the fine Miss Hawkins that she had helped him to change his mind about going out to her ranch. The first chance he got he would be out to check out her sick girls and a few other things.

Franklin went over to his cash box and emptied it into her hands. One of the old men in the waiting room saw Miss Sara Lee and just smiled. Two old gossiping church ladies saw her and just shook their heads and softly said, "There goes old Jezebel". A little boy asked his pa why the doctor was giving her all of his money. His pa just smiled said in time he'd find out. The boy said to his pa that there was a good smell in there. His pa asked what he was talking about. He asked his pa if he smelt that perfume and cinnamon.

As Miss Sara Lee was leaving out the door she looked over and saw Ruthie and David Burnstein. Mrs. Burnstein was trying to look down her nose at Sara Lee and Sara knew it but she spoke to her anyway. She said hello to Mrs. Burnstein then turned to her husband and said, "Hey there Dave, I ain't seen ya sense ya brought me that buffalo meat."

19
Home At Last

Master Rob had nicknamed his wife Manda and I loved to watch them 'sport' with one another from time to time.

As the morning sun peeped over the majestic stalks of corn, I saw a messenger riding in from town with a post for Amanda and Rob. Amanda read it and told me to show it to Rob when he came home for the evening meal. When Master Rob came in from the fields, I told him while he was out in the fields a messenger came by and left a message paper. He thanked me and teased me about my fat jaws.

Mr. Rob ran in the house looking for Amanda so she could read the message, however, Amanda had stepped out for a spell. He asked me where Ms. Amanda was.

I told him that she was at the little gal's house. This was the day he learned that the little gal's house and the toilet were one and the same. Then Mr. Rob tried making a play for me while his wife was gone.

Ms. Amanda came back inside of the house after she washed her hands in the horse trough and dried them off. Master Rob slid over and gave Ms. Amanda a little kiss on her lips. He started talking to her about the message and Amanda let him know that she had already read it. Rob begged her to read it again, this time so that he could hear it.

The message said that Jennifer, Amanda's sister, was coming back to stay.

Rob didn't believe his ears so he asked Ms. Amanda if it really said that. He wanted to know if the message said when she'd be arriving. The message was not specific, it only said in a few days.

It had been six or seven years since they last saw her or since she has run away. Amanda and Rob began to wonder if maybe Jennifer had gotten hitched. Their minds went back to the note that she had left under her pillow saying that she was in trouble but not with the law.

Rob and Amanda had but lost all hope of Jennifer really ever coming. It had been a full month or more and no Jennifer. One morning Amanda, Rob, Joeson and I were inside the house talking and a knock came on the door. I went to the door and opened it and there stood a little girl. The little child said is Ms. Amanda and Rob Henry there? When I asked her name, she said her name was Kateson.

I called to Mr. and Mrs. Henry that there was somebody out there that wanted to see them. They asked me who it was and a familiar voice came from the side of the house saying, "Why don't ya come see for yourself."

Ms. Amanda said, Lawd, it's my sister Jennifer's voice, I'd know it anywhere. Jennifer stepped from beside the house and came inside. Amanda, Rob and everybody began to hug her.

She told everybody to stop gawking at her and to help bring their bags inside. Master Rob asked her who that little child she had with her was. Jennifer told him that the child was hers.

Master Rob said, "Yours, what ya talking bout Jennifer, ain't no ways that can be your child!" The little child was dressed very fancy, just as pretty as any little white girl. She had on a pair of button up shoes and a blue satin dress. Her hair was all braided and dolled up with ribbons and bows.

Rob asked the little girl what her name was. She told him her name was Kateson and her mother's name was Ms Jennifer Shoesmith. She then asked

Master Rob what his name was. Ms. Amanda broke in telling the girl what a pretty child she was and told her that her name was Amanda and that she was pleased to meet her. When she asked Rob to agree with her on how pretty the little girl was, he simply committed that she was pretty to be 'one of them'. Ms. Amanda was putting it together that her name kind of sounded like Kate with son on the end. What could that possibly mean?

She asked Jennifer how old the child was. Jennifer said that if Amanda wasn't her sister, she would be mad with her. She asked Amanda to think about how long she had been gone.

Amanda answered saying about seven or eight years. She said that's how old my little girl is. Leave it to me to try to point out that the child was black, she told me to hush my mouth cause the child was listening.

She continued to ask them to stop gawking so much and help them take their bags upstairs. She told Joeson and Rob to hop to it. Joeson asked Ms. Amanda where she wanted him to put the child's bags. Jennifer asked him what he was talking about. She told him that the child was hers and she was going upstairs with her.

Rob questioned Jennifer because the child was . . . She said she knew what she was; she could see that for herself. She changed the subject to food and asked if they had anything to eat. Ms. Amanda told Joeson and me to go hustle up some food for the two.

They all sat at the table as the two guests began to eat. Amanda asked Jennifer where in the world she had been so long. Jennifer told Amanda that it seemed like she had been to hell and back. Amanda asked her why she would say that. She said that when she left there she had to find herself a job. The job she found was in a big hospital. Amanda asked her where the hospital was. She said she was still down South.

Amanda asked her why she didn't write or cable anybody because they never stopped loving her. She asked me to take her little girl upstairs and help her unpack their bags.

Amanda asked Jennifer to continue to talk her about her job. Jennifer wanted to wait until Kate came back downstairs so she could hear; her little girl could unpack by herself. They first wanted to know what all happened to Jennifer at that school she was at. They wanted to know about the trouble she had talked about having on the note she left under her bed pillow. Before she started talking about herself, she had a few questioned that she wanted to get answered.

Jennifer asked me where her husband, Old Joe was. She remembered that he always came to the door first to meet her at the door. Joeson began to look over at me as I sadly said that my husband, Old Joe, was dead and had been for a spell.

Jennifer said she was sorry and reached out to give me a hug and hold me a bit. She asked what happened. I told her that he died for the epidemic that was going around. Ms. Amanda urged Jennifer to move on from that conversation because it made me hurt so bad. Rob told Amanda to tell her about some of the folks she knew that had passed in the big sickness. Amanda agreed to tell her later.

Jennifer wanted to know what happened to that pretty woman, Miss Sara Lee Hawkins, cause when she and Kateson were coming there they passed by Old Turkey Creek and it looked like a fire had been there and no one was around. Amanda told her that was a long story too and she would tell her later. Next she asked

Joeson how he was doing. He said he was doing just fine.

Amanda began to tell Jennifer that Joeson had studied doctoring while she was gone and he took care of all of their sick folks and their neighbor's slaves too. Jennifer was impressed and wanted to know who taught him how to doctor folks. He told her that Doc Waters had taught him before he died. She wanted to know more about how Doc Waters died. They told her Doc Waters died from the same epidemic they mentioned before.

She wanted to know who the town doctor was now. Amanda wanted Jennifer to stop stalling and tell her where she had been for so long. Jennifer said okay but she just had one more question each for me and Joeson. She asked me if any other man had come calling on her since my man died.

I said no and asked Jennifer why she asked because she did not want to be bothered with no other man. I was getting riled up now. Jennifer said she asked because she thought I was still so pretty. I blushed a bit and told Jennifer that she could say some of the sweetest things.

She moved on to Joeson and asked him how many Joesons he had scattered over this plantation. He quickly said none that he knew about. She followed up by asking him if he had gotten hitched. His answer again was no.

"Well after I wrote ya last and told ya I was coming back I had a few hold ups."

They wanted to know what kind of holdups.

"Well ya see the stage coaches were cut off and stopped for a spell, because the Indians were beginning to raid and burn many of the small stations and out posts. When we arrived at two of the stations they were under Indian attack and we got out by the skin of our teeth."

They asked her if the Indians were up rising on all of the trails.

"They sure are, at least every where we been and seen, why?"

Rob said he needed to know because in the next few weeks he had to leave and go on a cattle drive and if what she was saying was true, it sounded powerfully scary to him.

"Well first of all let me start at one place at a time. When I was here last I did finish that nursing school I was attending. It finished bout two weeks before I left. When I realized that I was in trouble I was too afraid to tell anyone what had happened and I knew for sure ya wouldn't understand and ya probably would just hate me." (She began to cry.) *"And if ya only knew who it was that did it to me ya surely would have tried to kill him or hurt him some ways or another."*

Rob told her that he was her brother-in-law and she knew better than that. Amanda went over to her and hugged Jennifer and said that there was nothin she could ever do that would make her hate her.

"Sure ya say that Amanda, but ya really can't say that."

Rob said to her that there wasn't no need for crying because they always will love her and that she needed to believe that they would understand.

"Okay thanks for saying that Rob, but ya don't really know."

Amanda told her to calm herself down and asked Jennifer if she would tell her the truth if she asked a question of her.

"What's that Amanda?"

Amanda wanted to know who the man that got her in trouble was. Rob chirped in for Jennifer to say so that he could hide, heal, tar and feather him.

"Rob Henry, that's why I ain't gonna tell."

I came back to the table listening and the little girl was upstairs unpacking. I asked Jennifer who the little child belonged to.

Jennifer began to cry again.

"She mines. I had a child but it died at birth." *(she cried again)*

Amanda put her arms around her and patted her and cried some for her.

"It's okay." Jennifer says, *"Let me finish. At the hospital where I was working at many women would come and have their little babies. One afternoon I was headed home and a man ran up to me to come help him with one of his slave women that was about to have a baby. It had only been a few weeks after I had my baby that died. The poor slave woman died in childbirth.*

Her Master didn't want the child and he was going to leave it on the ground to die but I took it and gave it suck because my milk had not dried up and I fell in love with her and

*kept her. That little black child upstairs
is mines. Yes, she's mines I tell ya; And I
love her just like my own,"* (She began to cry
again) *"And I saw the look all of yawl had
when yawl first saw how she was all dressed up
like a little white child."*

Rob said it was okay with him if she loved
her as your own but he needed to get a little
drink because he thought the situation called
for a little drink.

*"Do ya want us to leave Mr. or Mrs. Rob
Henry because we will if you want us to!"*

Rob assured her that he didn't want her to
leave, she just got there.

As Rob was getting his drink Amanda said she
thought he had quit drinking that stuff. He
said he did but . . . He changed the attention
back to Jennifer. He wanted to make sure that
he had it straight.

She said she was pregnant and her child died
and she found a black slave woman having a baby
and she died and her Master left the baby to
die on the ground and that Jennifer took the
baby and let it put its nasty old black lips
and nurse and suck from your white breast.

*"Yes that's right Rob and I love that little
child!"*

Rob had one more question for Jennifer. He
asked why in Sam's Hell didn't she just leave
that baby there to die or at least give it to
some slave woman to raise.

*"Well to tell you the truth Mr. High And
Mighty, it was because I had compassion for
that poor little helpless child."* He accused
her of not knowing what she was doing.

"Amanda, I think me and my child, Kateson ain't welcomed here, so I guess I better be going."

Rob told her to sit herself down and that was always welcome at his house cause he loved her like her own sister. Rob kept saying that he had to get him a little drink. Rob looked at Jennifer and smiled and put his arms around her and told her to stop crying.

Kateson came downstairs and wanted to know what was going on. Rob picked Kateson up in his arms and he hugged her. He started talking to her and letting her know that he was her Uncle Rob.

"What ya dun said ya name twas Mr.?"

He told her his name was Rob and he was her uncle.

"No sir Mr. my Ma dun told me my Grandpas name is Rob, is there another Rob around here?"

He said no there wasn't and wanted to know what she was jabbering bout. Jennifer took her and told her to just hush. Rob said no, that he wanted to hear what she had to say. Jennifer told Rob to go on and get that drink he was talking about. Rob said okay to the drink and he left in a rush for town to get him a drink before they changed their minds.

After Rob left for town Amanda picked up Kateson and held her for a spell and said that the child sort of favored someone she had seen before but she just couldn't say who.

"Do I look like ya Ms. Amanda?"

Amanda asked her why she asked that.

"Cause Ms. Amanda ya pretty and I would be too."

She melted Amanda's heart with that one.

Amanda suggested to Jennifer that me and Joeson take her around the place and show her what was all new.

"Are ya sure Manda, I sure would be awfully appreciative to ya."

She said sure and kissed her sister on her cheek.

"Do ya want me to take Kateson with me?"

She told Jennifer she wanted to keep her for a spell and get to know her since she was going to be her new little friend.

I didn't like riding horseback, so Jennifer and Joeson took a small carriage from the barn and they went for a ride. While they were gone Amanda and Kateson had a long talk. Jennifer, me and Joeson came back from our ride and looking the plantation over. Amanda was talking and laughing with Kateson.

She told Jennifer that her little girl was a doll and she loved her as her own. She said she only wished her two children could have lived.

Now Jennifer was curious about what Amanda meant about her two children. Amanda told her that while she was gone that she got pregnant too. She story sadly went back to the time of the epidemic and that babies were coming from everywhere and she had a set of twins. She said she had named them Roberta and Robert.

Jennifer said she was sorry for Amanda's loss. Amanda said thanks but she at least knew for a few weeks what it felt like being a real mother before they both died of the whooping cough.

Jennifer held her and they both cried some together. Me and Joeson went and made them a pot of coffee. Amanda still cried from time to time and said her poor babies both died choking and strangling to death. Jennifer asked why she didn't try again to have another child. Amanda said they did but she came down with scarlet fever and a doctor once told her that because of it she would never have any more children.

Amanda broke loose from Jennifer's embrace and reframed herself and began laughing and said to Jennifer that she had something to confess to here.

"Why what's that big sister?"

Amanda confessed that while they were gone that Kateson and her had a big talk.

"Oh you did Amanda. Ain't she something else."

Amanda agreed. She continued by telling Jennifer that she put two and two together and got four from their talk. *"What ya talking bout Amanda?"*

Amanda said they should wait until I got back with the coffee.

I came back with the pot of coffee and Joeson brought two cups. Amanda told Joeson go get two more cups so they could have a drink of coffee.

Amanda sat at the table and gestured for me and Joeson to have a seat. Joeson could sense something was wrong but what he didn't rightly know. Joeson nervously asked Ms. Amanda didn't she think it was time for him to go out back and start taking care of the sick and ailing slave folk.

Amanda said it could wait and instructed him to pour them all a cup of coffee. He asked how everyone wanted their coffee. Amanda wanted her coffee black and I thought to myself that when Amanda drinks coffee with sugar every things alright but when she drinks black coffee look out something or somebody.

Amanda said now it was time for them to have a little talk. Kateson asked if she could go first. She was told no and it was best for her to go upstairs while grown folks talked alone. Amanda said "oh, no", Kateson is the reason why they were going to have this little talk in the first place.

Now everybody wanted to know what they were talking about.

"Well I'd just like to talk a few moments about something. Joeson I can recollect Master Henry had told me he had once asked ya if ya had ever been with any girl before."

Joeson smiled and said he could sort of recollect that some.

"What did ya tell him Joeson? Have you a little drink of coffee before you answer, because, I don't want you to lie to me boy."

Joeson said he could recollect telling him that he had once.

"Joeson you are sure telling the truth; but Joeson tell me the rest of the story." When Joeson said, yes, she asked him who was she. He said he wasn't going to tell, Amanda said to him, "Well son, I believe ya still telling me the truth. Joeson tell me son why didn't you tell who she was?"

Joeson said he was scared to death.

Amanda asked, *"Now why would he go and do a thing like that Joeson if ya were courting a slave girl like you ought to?"*

"Now Amanda, that ain't no business of yours", Jennifer said.

"Why not, Jennifer? Amanda asked. *I wonder if you might have something to hide too."*

"Oh now Amanda ya know good and well that's embarrassing don't ya!"

"Oh! You, Joeson I got another question to ask ya? When you laid with whoever it was, did ya really know what ya were doing and did ya know where babies came from?"

Joeson answered that he didn't at the time.

"How did ya find out where babies come from Joeson? Did your Ma tell ya, or did someone else tell you or show you?"

He said when he was with Doc Waters, one afternoon he saw a child being born into the world and he got terribly sick. Doc Waters had poked fun with him because he didn't know how it got inside of that gal's belly and he went home and told his folks and they both laughed some too. His Pa told him that evening where babies started from.

"Joeson man, how long was you on this here plantation before Waters trained you how to doctor folks?"

He responded with, "practically all his life ma'am, why?"

"Joeson", she laughed, *"ain't you or didn't you ever see the dogs, and cats out in the yards fooling around any?"*

He said well at times he did.

"Well man even as a young girl I used to ask my Ma and Pa why was that rooster hopping on the back of that hen and pecking her head and why the fillies would rare up after the stud horses got off of their backs? Joeson ain't ya ever walked into the room as a child when your Ma and Pa were locked together?"

Again, he said yes he did see some of that stuff before.

"But what did ya think was going on at that time, son?"

He said to tell the truth he really never did pay it no never mind.

"Joeson, tell me son, did ya ever see any other folks locked together and fouling around?"

Once again, he said yes a few times.

"Well would ya mind telling me who?"

He said he really didn't want to tell who.

"Why not, Joeson?" Jennifer asked.

He told Jennifer it might be slighty embarrassing.

"Oh, Joeson man, go ahead on and tell it can't be that embarrassing, can it?"

"Well ma'am once when I was nothin but a little buck my Ma had asked me to go out to the smokehouse and get some pork meat to cook the beans with and I had opened the door all quiet like and dun saw two white folks over in the straw and, and . . ."

"And what, Joeson?"

"Well ma'am I closed the door in a quick hurry like?"

"Joeson don't tell no more, Amanda said.

Why not Manda, I want to hear the rest of this. Who was it Joeson, Jennifer asked?

"Ain't none of your business, that's why Jennifer Shoesmith."

"Hey here now sister dear it ain't no cause for you to get so riled up is there, or is there. Hum Amanda from the look on your face I can sense who it was, Joeson go ahead on and tell."

"No Jennifer I don't want to hear."

"Why not Manda if it wasn't you, well then just who in the world you think it might be. Kate, do ya know?"

I said I didn't know who it was.

Jennifer said, "Joeson come here man and whisper in my ear who it was."

He whispered and she began laughing and said,

"Why Amanda Henry I never dreamed you would ever do such a thing, shame . . . shame . . . shame. I knew old Perry Joe Blackberry had moved out this ways but you never told me he was coming by to see ya."

Amanda asked Joeson why he whispered and told Jennifer about Perry. I asked if they was talking about the watermelon man that brought by the melons every crop time.

Jennifer smiled and said, "Oh, Kate let me tell you honey. When we lived out West, him and Manda were once engaged but they broke up because . . ."

"Now Jennifer you hush up your mouth, you just make me sick talking, so much.

Let's get back to what I was going to talk about before."

"What you talking about Amanda?"

"Jennifer I told you I done put two and two together."

"What you talking about Amanda Henry?"

"Now, Joeson, back to my question. What was the girl's name that you done been with? But before you tell me her name, tell me something Joeson?"

He trembled and shook in fear and asked what she wanted to know.

"Joeson did you lay with this somebody before my sister Jennifer left and ran away?"

He said he did. He looked over at me and tears began to well up in his eyes.

"Jennifer, tell us something?"

"What's that sister dear?"

"Can you tell the truth and tell me how many men you had been with before you left here and why you named your child Kateson?"

"Sure I can tell you I only been with one man in my whole life. But what's that got to do with who Joeson done laid with?"

"Just ya wait and in time you'll see."

"Well go ahead on Lawyer and Judge Amanda Henry."

"Jennifer was he at that school you were attending or was he from some other plantation and could he have been black?"

"Now Amanda Henry, aren't you ashamed?"

"I ain't gonna tell!"

"Why?"

"Well tell me then, Jennifer, is that man sitting at this table?"

"I'm not going to say. You know something Amanda, when, we were kids you always said if

234

you were a man you would like to be a lawyer and study law."

"You really don't have to answer my question Jennifer because while you were gone I asked Kateson if she knew who her real Ma and Pa was and she told me that her real Ma was you but I didn't take the child serious until I asked her did she know who her pa was and she said you had told her that her real pa was the son of Kate, a slave woman that she had once knew.

When she said that I began to cry, because I had figured out why she was named Kateson. You named her after the person you had loved, didn't ya Jennifer? Your little girl was named after her real Pa."

I questioned Ms. Amanda about what she was saying because I didn't quite understand.

"Yeah, Amanda Henry, if you wasn't my sister I'd say you're trying to insinuate something dirty?"

"Jennifer I ain't no fool you know, I got your letter put up in a box upstairs and every so often I read it."

"What you talking Amanda?"

"Jennifer your letter said something like this: 'If I have this child I'll name it after the people I love.' Jennifer between me and you, Kateson ain't or never was any slave woman's child was she?"

Ms. Amanda asked me to pour her a cup of that black coffee again. "Jennifer, tell me the truth gal. Ain't Kateson your real child?"

Jennifer began crying and said, "Yes she is Amanda, Yes she is, she's my child."

Jennifer rushed over to Kateson and hugged her tightly.

I said, *Oh my Lawd give me a drink of that there black coffee*, and urged Joeson to take his cup too. Joeson asked me why he needed some coffee. I told him because she thought that Kateson was his child. Then I passed out on the floor and fainted.

Amanda told Joeson go upstairs quickly and look inside her closet and get her smelling salts because his Ma had passed out from all the excitement. They put the salts *under my nose and I came back around.*

Amanda said, "Kate, now gal you can stop sweating so hard and put sugar in all of our cups."

I asked Amanda if she was saying that everything was going to be okay.

"Sure it is, Sure it is, even better than you think."

Joeson had tears in his eyes and was puzzled about what Ms. Amanda was saying because he just knew that if Master Henry found out that he would surely kill him.

"Oh don't worry Joeson, Master Rob ain't gonna kill you, just you wait and see." Joeson told Ms. Amanda that he knew he would be as good as dead if other white folks found out that he had been with a white woman.

"I know Joeson, but they ain't gonna find out cause ya just don't know how long your Master has been wanting to see a grandchild born of his blood."

"What ya talking about Amanda, now ya got me puzzled, if ya and hem ain't got no children how can he have grandchildren?"

"How do ya think Jennifer? A man can have children outside of his wife ya know. Kate haven't ya ever told Joeson who his real Pa is?"

I said, no I hadn't. Amanda asked her why not. I said that she always thought the Amanda would get fighting mad at her.

Jennifer said, "Amanda what ya talking about?"

Amanda answered, "Jennifer in case ya don't already know my husband, Rob Henry is Joeson's real Pa."

Joeson was in shock and grabbed a cup of coffee and a whole lot of sugar.

I looked over at my son and almost fainted again but Jennifer put more of the salts under my nose.

Joeson asked Amanda if she realized what she just said.

"Sho I do Joeson. I just said Rob Henry is your real Pa."

"He is?"

"Here Jennifer don't you start fainting too; here take yourself a sniff of this smelling salts and while you're at it, let me have me a smell! Yeah he sure is son. He's your real Pa."

Joeson said that he thought his real pa was Old Joe. I said he was and she probably should have told him before now but she didn't think he would understand. Jennifer told Kateson to go upstairs to their room and take nap. The child said okay but she wished she could hear more.

"Now that Kateson has gone upstairs, I got something to tell all of you."

"What's that big sister?"

"Jennifer after you left I just cried and cried because I missed you so bad. Jennifer did you know that our Ma had died the year after you had left?"

"No I didn't know (She cried some) but after my child was born I did go home and let Ma see her."

"You did?"

"Well did she know?"

"Of course she did."

"And what did she say?"

"She was tickled to death and she loved the child with all of her heart."(She cried again).

"Oh Amanda, what have I done?"

"Now, now Jennifer calm down because I got something to tell you." Jennifer, Rob and I had an idea that Joeson was the father of your child but wasn't for sure."

"What are you talking, Amanda Henry?"

"You see Jennifer, when you left Rob and I had talked at night bout you."

"What kind of talks?"

"Well you see Jennifer when you wrote and said what you had said, at first I thought you had gotten in trouble by that Corn fellow you had went out with a few times but Rob only laughed and said ain't no ways you really took that joker seriously."

"Well who did you all think it was?"

"Well to tell you the truth we really didn't know who it was but we both knew you had feelings for Joeson even thought you were trying to keep it hidden."

"*What you saying Amanda?*"

"*Now, Jennifer, Rob and I ain't crazy!*"

"*So, what you telling me Amanda?*"

"*I'm telling you Jennifer Shoesmith that the looks on both of your faces told us.*"

"*Oh come on now Amanda.*"

"*Jennifer don't ya remember our Pa used to say that a look can say a thousand words.*" I wanted Amanda to explain why she said Master Henry wouldn't hurt Joeson?

"*Kate don't worry Master Henry already knows Joeson is the father of Jennifer's child.*"

Kate wanted to know how he knew that. "*First of all Joeson and Kate let me tell the both of you something I've never told any of you before. Rob really ain't as bad as all of you think he is or he seems to be.*"

Kate agreed that she had seen that for herself.

"*Hold on now Kate and let me finish. Jennifer, honey I might have told you before that Rob's old Pa, Old man Henry, first owned this plantation and before he died he gave it to Rob. Rob really didn't want it at first, because he simply hated the idea of slavery and having slaves.*"

Joeson asked why that was.

"*Cause Joeson your Master, Master Henry had other brothers and sisters.*"

Joeson asked why he never talked about them. "*Well to tell you the truth about it Jennifer, he is somewhat ashamed of what his Pa had done.*"

"*What you talking about Amanda Henry?*"

"*Well you see Jennifer Rob's other brothers and sister was half white and half black.*"

"*What, what ya say Amanda?*"

"*You heard what I said. Now Kate close your mouth and Joeson you too. I said your Master has half white brothers and sisters and he never wanted them to be mistreated.*"

"*Amanda Henry you just got to slow up a bit and tell me more.*"

"*Okay Jennifer I know this comes as a shock to you but it's really true.*" Joeson asked Amanda that if Master Henry had other brothers and sisters then why didn't they ever come around.

"*Well you see Joeson it's because the number one reason is because Rob would be ashamed if any other white folks found out or knew and the other reason is because when Rob took over this plantation they were still living here before I ever married him and he set them all free and sent them all up North to live.*"

Jennifer wanted to know if he had ever seen anymore since he set them free. "*Well to tell you the truth Jennifer, yes he has; every so often he goes to visit them.*"

Joeson said 'My Lawd, My Lawd' and asked Amanda if he could ask another question. She told him to go ahead and ask. He wanted to know why Master Henry sold them off if he cared so much.

"*Oh Joeson come here son and let me hold you for a minute and stop your crying man. Joeson, Rob has to make a living and how he does it is by running a plantation.*" I said I understood that but I wanted to know why he was so hard on them at times.

"*Kate, believe me when I tell you that he ain't as hard as you think sometimes.*"

She said yes he was because she could still recall how he sold off some of the slaves and they never saw them anymore.

"*Kate I got a secret to tell you. Have you ever noticed when some of you folks get old or hurt and you can't work he always get rid of you? Well you see things ain't what they seem cause he really don't be selling them folks off Rob takes them to the depot and pays for them a ticket for up North and some he just lets go free.*"

"*But how do they make it Amanda, if they ain't got nothin?*"

"*Jennifer, Rob sends them away with money to live with for at least three years.*"

"*He does?*"

"*Yes he does Jennifer and Jennifer ain't you ever noticed if any of his white helpers ever hurt or mistreat any of his slaves and he finds out he usually will fire them or let them go.*"

Joeson said that he had noticed that before but he didn't ever know why. He asked Amanda did Master Rob tell her that he was his pa.

"*No he didn't Joeson.*"

Joeson was confused about how she knew if Master Rob didn't tell her.

"*Well Joeson, no one ever told me because I just knew.*"

You just knew! But how Amanda Henry did ya know?"

"*Jennifer a woman just knows. Didn't I just tell you a spell ago that a look can say a thousand words.*"

"*Well yes you did, but you still ain't telling me nothin.*"

"Jennifer I wasn't there when Kate got caught but I certainly was there when she gave birth to Joeson and I remember the look on Kate's face when I asked her what she wanted to name her son and she looked at Rob and said she wanted to name him after his Pa and she was crying. I saw the look of guilt on Rob Henry's face but Old Joe named him after himself."

"But how did you know Amanda Henry? You still ain't never told me how you knew."

"It's because Joeson may be black and a slave, but he looks just like his Pa Rob Henry. Joeson told her to wait a minute.

"No Joeson, son, ya wait a minute. I'm telling you Rob Henry is your pa and because of it that's why he ain't going to hurt you for being with Jennifer. Now Joeson tell me son, why do ya think I sometimes call ya son?

He said because he guessed it was because she liked him some.

"Joeson you're so silly at times. Son you really are my son and I do really love you."

Now he questioned her because Kate was his ma and how could he have two mas.

"Joeson don't forget you got two pas too, or should I say you had two, but one is dead now." I asked Amanda what they were gonna do about Jennifer and Kateson.

"Well Kate I'm going to ask you something. What did I make a few of the other slaves around here do that got caught doing the horse?"

Joeson began laughing and said she made them both jump the broom.

So what ya think I'm going to make Jennifer and the man she had Kateson by do?"

Joeson admitted that he didn't know. They had to put the smelling salts under his nose after she told him.

The End

I know you would like to know how a slave man living in the South could marry a white woman and not be killed. I would like to tell you but that's going to be my next novel. I love you and may "The Good Lord Bless You All."

Acknowledgement

The handsome looking old gentleman `whose picture is featured is my granddad.

I do want you to know that I am the great grandson of a former slave named Mr. John Grayham. I would like to acknowledge my grandfather for being the person that told me some of the true tales about slavery.

Granddad's name was Mr. Ulysis Grayham. He had told me before that he had nineteen brother and sisters. His parents had twenty children including him. My granddad was married to my grandmother, Myrtis who gave birth to eleven children. Eight of their children died as young babies. Only three of their children survived. My mother, her older sister and a younger brother were the survivors. These three are now all deceased.

My grandfather had told me when I was a youngster how he had entered the Army when he was only fifteen years old and how he was one of the original buffalo soldiers. Gramps told me how his pa, Mr. John Grayham, was twenty-one years old when slavery was abolished. When my mother, Ms. Johnnie Mae McClure was alive, she told me that she had seen both of her dad's parents.

My granddad lived to be one hundred and eight years old. If he were still here, I would let him know that I will always love him and this book is dedicated to his memory. Many of the tales he once told me and my younger sister Francis are contained within these pages.

I would like to thank my wife and all of my children for always being there for me while I was trying to write and get this book published.

Most of all I would like to thank my wife for always encouraging me not to give up when the going got rough. Thanks for all of your support and prayers.

I would also like to give thanks to all of my family members both far and near that gave me the little push I needed. Before my mom died, I let her read a part of my story and tears welled in her eyes and she asked,

"Junior, daddy told you that story, didn't he?" I just smiled and "said yes he did mama, yes he did."

I would also like to thank Ms. Micky Pickens of JOAT-LLC Consulting for her work as my ghost writer and coordinator through this journey to publication.

Image Credits

Thanks to my family members and to the following entities for the use of the images in this book:

Chapter 3: Mr. Tom's Death:
"Funeral, Paramaribo, Suriname", 1831, Image Reference BEN-15a as shown on www.hitchcock. itc.virginia.edu/Slavery/details.php?catego rynum=14&categoryName=Religion and Mortuary Practices & the Record

Chapter 11: "Sisters"
"Madagascar Women-1850s", Image Reference Ellis-161 as shown on www.slaveryimages.org, compiled by Jerome Handler and Michael Tuite, and sponsored by the Virginia Foundation for the Humanities and the University of Virginia Library.

Chapter 15: "Doc Joeson"
Family picture of my (author's) father

Chapter 18: "Miss Sara Lee"
Photo Products, Pittsburg KS

Chapter 19: "Home at Last-A"
"Black Nursemaid," New Orleans, 1873-74", Image
Reference King01 as shown on http://hitchcock.
itc.virginia.edu/Slavery. Edward King, The
Great South (Hartford, Conn., 1875), p. 30
(Special Collections, University of Virginia
Library)

Chapter 19: "Home at Last-B"
Family picture of my (author's) sister

Acknowledgement: Family picture of my (author's)
grandfather